We hope you enjoy
Please return or ren
You can renew it at   **ries**
or by using our free library app.   can
phone **0344 800 8020** - please have your library
card and pin ready.
You can sign up for email reminders too.

D0513067

-H

11. 10. 21		

NORFOLK COUNTY COUNCIL
LIBRARY AND INFORMATION SERVICE

NORFOLK ITEM

3 0129 08546 1904

Look out for all of these enchanting story collections

by *Enid Blyton*

Animal Stories
Cherry Tree Farm
Christmas Stories
Christmas Tales
Christmas Treats
Christmas Wishes
Fireworks in Fairyland
Magical Fairy Tales
Mr Galliano's Circus
Nature Stories
Rainy Day Stories
Springtime Stories
Stories of Magic and Mischief
Stories of Rotten Rascals
Stories of Wizards and Witches
Summer Adventure Stories
Summer Holiday Stories
Summertime Stories
Tales of Tricks and Treats
The Wizard's Umbrella
Winter Stories

Enid Blyton

STORIES OF SPELLS AND ENCHANTMENTS

Illustrations by Mark Beech

HODDER CHILDREN'S BOOKS

This collection first published in Great Britain in 2021
by Hodder & Stoughton

1 3 5 7 9 10 8 6 4 2

A CIP catalogue record for this book is available from the British Library.

ISBN 978 1 444 96200 0

Typeset by Avon DataSet Ltd, Arden Court, Alcester, Warwickshire

Printed and bound in Great Britain by Clays Ltd, Elcograf S.p.A.

The paper and board used in this book are made from
wood from responsible sources.

Hodder Children's Books
An imprint of Hachette Children's Group
Part of Hodder & Stoughton
Carmelite House
50 Victoria Embankment
London EC4Y 0DZ

An Hachette UK Company
www.hachette.co.uk
www.hachettechildrens.co.uk

Contents

The Enchanted Bellows

The Enchanted Bellows

ONCE UPON a time there were two little imps called Bubble and Squeak. They lived in Puff Cottage, and they made bellows. They sold them for a penny each, and made quite a lot of money. They carved animals on the handles, and all the fairies came to buy them because they were so well made and pretty.

Now Bubble was good and Squeak was naughty. Squeak was always trying to make Bubble do things he shouldn't, but usually Bubble wouldn't do them. Then one day Squeak had a very strange idea.

'Bubble!' he said in an excited whisper. 'Let's get a wind spell from the Blowaway Witch, and put it into a pair of bellows! Then we'll sell them to someone we don't like, and see what happens!'

'Don't be naughty,' said Bubble. 'And stop whispering in my ear like that. It tickles.'

'But Bubble, oh Bubble, do let's!' said Squeak. 'It's the loveliest idea I've ever had. Just think how funny it would be to put a spell into a pair of bellows! Why, they'd blow and blow and blow all by themselves, and it would be such a joke.'

Squeak began to laugh, and when he laughed Bubble simply had to do the same, because Squeak's laugh went on and on like a bubbling stream. And as soon as Bubble began to laugh he felt just as naughty as Squeak.

'All right,' he said, when he had got his breath again. 'Let's go to the Blowaway Witch now, before I change my mind.'

So off they went. The Blowaway Witch lived on the top of a steep hill, and was friends with the South Wind. There was always a breeze round her cottage, and her chimney smoke never went straight up into the sky. It was always blown this way and that.

The two imps were very much out of breath when they at last reached the cottage. They knocked at the door, and the witch came to open it.

'What do you want?' she said.

'Please could you let us have a wind spell?' asked Squeak.

'What for?' asked the witch.

'To put into one of our pairs of bellows,' said Bubble, going red.

'But that would be naughty,' said the witch. 'Besides, the spell is sixpence, and I am sure you haven't so much money as that.'

'Yes, we have,' said Squeak, and he took out a bright new sixpence. 'Please let us have the spell, dear witch.'

Just at that moment the South Wind came to the door too, for he happened to be having tea with the Blowaway Witch, and had heard all that the imps had said.

'Give them the spell,' he said. 'They can't do any harm with it!'

So the witch took down her box of spells, and looked inside for a wind spell. She took out one that was not very strong, but just as she was going to hand it to Bubble, she dropped it. The South Wind picked it up, but before he gave it to the imps he breathed on it.

That will make it ten times as strong as the strongest wind spell that ever was made! he thought to himself in glee, for he was a very mischievous fellow. *They will get more than they bargain for! What fun!*

The two imps knew nothing of this. They took the spell, said thank you, paid the witch, and went off down the hill. When they got home they made a fine pair of bellows with ducks carved on the handle, and then with much laughter they pushed the wind spell right into the very middle of the bellows.

'Now as soon as anyone uses these, the wind spell will start working, and blow everything all about the room!' chuckled Bubble and Squeak. 'Ooh, wouldn't we like to see it!'

They wondered who would buy the bellows, and they decided to wait until someone they didn't like at all came along. And that someone arrived the very next day.

It was Grunts, the old gnome from the bluebell wood. He was very bad-tempered and rude, and the imps disliked him very much. So they thought they would sell him the enchanted bellows.

'My bellows are broken,' said Grunts. 'I want a new pair. Show me some.'

So the imps showed him a lot, and then they took out the enchanted pair. The ducks on the handle were beautifully carved, and Grunts liked them.

'How much are these?' he asked.

'Only a ha'penny,' said Squeak. 'The others are all a penny each.'

'Then I'll take the ha'penny pair,' said Grunts, and he put a bent and battered half penny down on the counter. Bubble wrapped the bellows up in brown paper, and gave them to the gnome.

Off he went, and the two imps looked at one another and laughed.

'Let's follow him and see what happens!' said Bubble, feeling very naughty indeed.

So they followed Grunts to his home in the bluebell wood. He lived not far away from the palace of the fairy king and queen, and had a very nice little cottage. He was one of the gardeners and kept the grounds of the palace in good order.

Now just as he had nearly reached his home, with the imps close behind him following quietly in his footsteps, someone came running to meet Grunts.

'The queen wants you!' panted the messenger. 'She wants some extra special roses for a dinner party tonight, and says will you please pick them now?'

'I'll go straight to the palace,' said Grunts. So, instead of going home, he turned to the right, and took the path that led to the palace garden. The imps went too, for they thought they would like to see the roses.

Grunts went in at a little green gate, and picked the roses for the queen. Just as he had finished gathering a beautiful bunch, Her Majesty came down the path.

'Oh thank you, Grunts,' she said. 'I'll take them in myself. Oh dear me, what's this?'

She had nearly fallen over the brown parcel in which the bellows were. Grunts had put it down on the grass while he picked the roses.

'I beg your pardon, Your Majesty,' he said. 'Those are my new bellows.'

'Oh, *could* you lend me them for a moment?' asked the queen. 'The fire in the drawing room wants a good blowing, and we can't find the bellows anywhere.'

'Certainly, Your Majesty,' said Grunts. 'Pray let me come and do it for you.'

He picked up the bellows, and walked down the path with the queen. The two imps were full of horror. Oh dear, oh dear! Whatever would happen in the palace when the bellows blew! They ran after the queen and Grunts, meaning to beg them not to use the bellows.

But they were too late. Grunts was kneeling down by the fire, blowing hard with the bellows, when the two imps looked in at the window.

Then things began to happen. Suddenly a loud wheezing sound came from the bellows, and they leapt right out of Grunts' hands. They worked themselves, and a great wind came out of them. It blew all the roses out of the vase that the queen had put them in. Then it blew all the newspapers out of the rack, and puffed the curtains right out of the window.

'Oh, oh!' cried the queen. 'Whatever is happening? Take the bellows outside, Grunts! There is something wrong with them!'

But Grunts couldn't catch them! They went flying all over the place, blowing for all they were worth. Puff-puff-puff! And off went the cushions from the couch, and into the air went the tablecloth! The cat was blown right off her chair, and the dog sailed out of the room backwards. The queen's lovely golden hair was blown all about her face, and she had to hold tightly to the mantelpiece to prevent herself from being blown out of the window!

'Ooh!' cried Bubble and Squeak, as the bellows suddenly puffed at them. Off they went, blown backwards, rolling over and over. Then they sat up and looked at one another.

Bubble began to cry.

'I do wish we hadn't been naughty,' he sobbed. 'Look what's happened now! Whoever would have thought that the Blowaway Witch would have sold us such a strong spell for sixpence. And it's getting stronger every minute!'

So it was. The bellows made a much louder noise now, and blew so strongly that even chairs and tables went rolling over. Then the bellows flew out into the hall, and met a footman carrying a tray of cups and plates. Every single one was blown into the air, and came down in pieces. As for the poor footman, he was blown to the end of the hall, and knocked the king himself over.

'Now what's this, what's this?' cried the king in a temper. 'What do you mean by tearing about backwards like this, footman?'

But just then the bellows came near and – puff! The king himself was blown into the air and bumped his head against the ceiling. He caught hold of a swinging lantern, and hung there, very much frightened. The footman ran to get a ladder to help him down.

What a to-do there was in the palace! The king shouted, the queen cried, the footman rushed here and there trying to catch the bellows, and the cook threw a saucepan at them, but only managed to hit the butler, who was very angry.

The bellows thoroughly enjoyed themselves. They sent a large bed sailing into the garden, and went out after it. Then they blew two chimney pots off the roof, and puffed so hard at a gardener that he found himself sitting at the top of a beech tree before he knew what was happening.

Grunts was filled with amazement. How could his pair of bellows be so wicked? Hadn't he bought them for a ha'penny that day from Bubble and Squeak? Surely they couldn't have put such a strong spell into them?

As for Bubble and Squeak, they were shaking and trembling, for they knew that they would be found out and punished sooner or later. Whatever would the queen say to them? And how could that dreadful pair of bellows be stopped?

'Let's run to the Blowaway Witch and ask her what to do!' said Bubble, with tears running down his turned-up nose. So off they went.

They didn't stop once till they reached the witch's cottage. Then they banged on her door.

When she came, they told her all that had happened.

'The king was blown up to the ceiling, and the

gardener sailed up to the top of the beech tree, and all the cups and saucers and plates flew into the air off the footman's tray!' sobbed Bubble. 'Oh, whatever are we to do? We didn't know you had given us such a strong wind spell, witch. How can we stop it?'

The witch went very pale, and sat down suddenly.

'*I* didn't give you a strong spell,' she said. 'I gave you the weakest one I had, for I was afraid you were up to mischief, as usual. What *can* have happened to it?'

'Do you suppose the South Wind did anything to your spell?' asked Squeak. 'He was here when you sold it to us, you know.'

'So he was,' said the witch, jumping up. 'Well, I'll get him here, and ask him.'

She took an old tea tray out to her garden, and banged it with an iron spoon. In three minutes the South Wind came rushing down.

'What do you want?' he asked. 'I heard you calling me.'

The witch told him all that had happened at

the palace, and the South Wind looked most uncomfortable.

'Yes,' he said. 'I breathed on the spell and made it very strong indeed – VERY strong indeed – but of course I hadn't any idea at all that the queen herself would ask for the bellows to be used in the palace. I thought perhaps some old gnome or goblin would get a shock, that's all.'

'Well, what are we to do?' asked the imps.

'I and the South Wind will come with you and see if we can stop the bellows from blowing,' said the witch. She put on her best cloak, climbed on her broomstick, took the two imps behind her, and then set off with the South Wind to the palace.

When they arrived there, they found the enchanted bellows still blowing everywhere. The king's crown had been blown to the top of a chimney, and six hens had been puffed up to the highest tower of the palace. It was dreadful.

The witch hastily drew a circle of white chalk, and

stepped inside it. Then she chanted a long string of magic words, beckoning the bellows towards her all the time. Little by little they stopped blowing, and came towards the witch. As soon as they were near the magic circle, she reached out her hand and grabbed them. Once they were in the circle all their enchantment left them, and they became ordinary bellows.

'Well, they're cured now,' said the witch, and she stepped out of her circle. She went to the queen, and told her everything that had happened to make the bellows behave so strangely.

The king and queen were very angry. 'The imps had no right to play tricks like that,' they said, 'and as for the South Wind, he ought to be ashamed of himself for his share in this terrible muddle. Just look at the palace! All upside down and topsy-turvy! He shall be banished from Fairyland for a whole year, and he can take those mischievous imps with him!'

Very sorrowfully the South Wind went away, and

the two imps followed him, weeping bitterly. The footman picked up the bellows and threw them after the imps – and as soon as they left the magic circle, their enchantment came back. They began to blow and blow again, and the two imps flew straight up into the air, and found themselves in the clouds.

The South Wind caught the bellows and gave them to the imps. 'I will look after you and be your friend,' he said, 'but you must work for me in return. Sometimes I can't be bothered to blow the clouds along on a summer's day, because I'm too sleepy. You can blow them for me with these bellows.'

And that is what Bubble and Squeak do now. If you see the clouds sailing slowly along on a summer's day when there is no breeze, you will be able to guess what is happening – the South Wind is fast asleep somewhere, and the two imps are puffing the clouds along with the bellows. They hope to go back to Fairyland some day, and if they are good, I expect they will.

Mr Tweeky's Magic Pockets

Mr Tweeky's
Magic Pockets

MR TWEEKY was a round, little man, with the jolliest smile you could imagine. He was dreadfully poor, and he lived all by himself in a round, little cottage at the end of Dum-Dum Village. He always wore a red coat that buttoned tightly up to his neck and had two very deep pockets in it. In one of them he kept his dinner, and in the other he put things like handkerchiefs, money and tickets.

One day Mr Tweeky started off to look for work. He had a very dull dinner wrapped up in paper in one of his pockets, and he wasn't looking forward to eating it. He hoped perhaps he would be able to find some work, and then he might buy a nice bit of cheese to go with his dry bread.

He was just going down the road when he heard someone call, 'Help! Help!' He looked to see who it was, and saw an old woman waving to him out of a window.

'A pipe has burst in the bathroom, and the house is being swamped!' she cried. 'Come and help me, do!'

Mr Tweeky rushed into the house. He took his coat off in the hall, and hung it up, with his hat. Then he turned up his shirt sleeves and tore upstairs.

Dear me! What a sight he saw! The water was pouring out of a hole in a pipe and had soaked everything.

'I'll put my thumb on it while you go for a plumber,' said Mr Tweeky. 'Hurry up, or you'll have to swim!'

'Thank you, thank you,' said the old woman, and

she ran downstairs. Mr Tweeky waited for about twenty minutes with his thumb on the hole, and then the old woman came back with a plumber who quickly stopped the water and said he would put in a new piece of pipe.

'I'm very grateful to you,' said the old woman to Mr Tweeky. 'Thank you so much.'

'Don't mention it,' said Mr Tweeky politely. 'I'm glad to have been of use. I'll just pop downstairs now and get my coat.'

So down he popped and put on his coat and hat once more. Then out into the street he went, whistling cheerily, glad that he had been able to do someone a good turn.

'Hallo, Tweeky!' said a friend of his. 'Where have you been?'

Mr Tweeky told his friend about the burst pipe.

'You're a good chap,' said his friend Higgle, who was very fond of Mr Tweeky. 'I wish you could get a bit of good luck. You are always poor, and you never have any treats.'

'Ah,' said Mr Tweeky, sighing, 'I wish the good old days of fairies would come back again. Then I'd wish a few wishes, and get everything I wanted!'

Higgle walked along with Mr Tweeky, and when dinnertime came they sat down together on a sunny bank to eat their meal. Mr Tweeky's friend had cold sausage and new bread and a nice piece of cake.

'What have *you* got, Tweeky?' he asked.

'Only stale, dry bread, and not very much of that!' said Mr Tweeky, sighing again. 'I wish I'd got cold sausage and new bread like you. And for my pudding I'd like a nice piece of jam roll.'

He put his hand in his pocket and pulled out his dinner. It was wrapped up in paper. Mr Tweeky unwrapped it – and then he stared as if he couldn't believe his eyes!

'Buttons and buttercups!' he cried. 'Look here! Here's my wish come true, I do declare! Cold sausage! New bread! And – oh! The finest piece of jam roll I

24

ever saw! Why, there's magic about still!'

Mr Tweeky's friend stared with his eyes and mouth wide open. He thought it was a most surprising thing.

Mr Tweeky ate up his dinner with joy. He had never had such a delicious one before. The jam roll was perfectly lovely, and the sausage was really tasty.

'You've got jam all over your nose and mouth,' said Higgle. 'You do look funny.'

Mr Tweeky dived into his other pocket for his handkerchief – but when he brought it out he was lost in astonishment.

'Look at that!' he shouted in delight. 'My own handkerchief is an old, torn red cotton one – and it's changed into this lovely blue silk one! Buttons and buttercups, there's certainly magic about today!'

'That's a wonderful thing,' said Higgle. 'Well, Tweeky, I always said you deserved a bit of good luck if ever anyone did – and now that you've got it, I'm glad.'

Mr Tweeky beamed all over his round, little face. He was so pleased. He wiped the jam off his nose and put his handkerchief away again.

'Well, I must go on now,' he said. 'I heard that there was a gardener wanted at the other end of the village. I must go and see if I can get the job.'

'I'm going that way too,' said Higgle, 'but I'm going to take the bus – it's so far to walk.'

'I haven't enough money for that,' said Mr Tweeky, putting his hand into his pocket. 'Look, I've only got twopence!'

He pulled out a coin – and my, didn't he stare! It was a shilling!

'Look at that now!' he said. 'There's my twopence changed into a shilling! Did you ever see anything like it?'

Higgle was more surprised than ever. He took the shilling and bit it to see if it was good, and it was.

'Now you'll be able to catch the bus,' he said. 'The fare is only threepence.'

So they both caught the bus, and Mr Tweeky enjoyed the ride very much, for it was a long time since he had been in a bus.

'Would you like a toffee?' asked Higgle. 'I've got one to spare.'

'Oh, that's very kind of you,' said Mr Tweeky. 'I wish I'd a few to offer you, but I haven't a single one.'

'I say! Feel in your pockets and see if you've got any now!' said Higgle excitedly. So Mr Tweeky felt solemnly in his pockets – and brought out a whole bag of assorted toffees!

'Well, I never!' he said. 'This is the loveliest day I've ever had, Higgle. My luck certainly *is* in.'

'See what else you've got in your pockets,' said Higgle. 'Perhaps everything has changed into something better.'

So Mr Tweeky looked – and he was *so* astonished at what he found. First there was a very nice pair of gloves, with fur inside. Then there was another handkerchief, made of yellow silk. There were two

27

lovely pencils and a fine fountain pen. There was a notebook, a purse with five shillings in, and, last of all, a little case.

'What's in the case?' asked Higgle, bending over to see. 'My, Tweeky, there's certainly plenty of magic about you today!'

Mr Tweeky opened the case. Inside there were a lot of visiting cards.

'Oh, fancy!' he cried. 'These are cards! I expect they'll all have my name on! Buttons and buttercups! How grand I shall be!'

He took out one of the cards and looked at it – and then he looked again – and then he rubbed his eyes and looked a third time.

'Look, Higgle,' he said to his friend. 'Do you see my name there?'

Higgle looked. 'No!' he said in surprise. 'It's someone else's name! It says Mr Joseph Hubble-Bubble! Now, whatever does that mean?'

'Well, my name's Tweeky, isn't it?' said Mr

Tweeky, puzzled. 'Something's gone wrong with the magic. I wonder why they put Hubble-Bubble.'

'There's a Mr Hubble-Bubble who lives in the village somewhere,' said Higgle. 'I've heard of him. I wonder why his name is on the cards in your pocket. This is very funny.'

Then a really terrible thought came to Mr Tweeky. He turned quite pale. He looked down at his red coat, and turned paler still. He quite frightened Higgle.

'What's the matter?' said his friend. 'Are you ill, Tweeky?'

'No,' said Tweeky in a faint voice. 'But, oh, Higgle! I don't believe these pockets are magic, after all. I-I-I—'

'What! Tell me quickly!' cried Higgle.

'I-I-I-believe I've got someone else's coat on,' said poor Mr Tweeky. 'I hardly dare to look, Higgle. Just tell me, is there a big patch on the right shoulder?'

Higgle looked. 'No,' he said. 'There's no patch at all.'

'Is there a button gone from the right cuff?' asked Mr Tweeky.

'No, there's a button there all right,' said Higgle.

'Then it's n-n-n-not my coat,' said Mr Tweeky. 'Oh, what shall I do?'

'But how could you have got someone else's?' asked Higgle, puzzled.

'Why, do you remember that I told you how I went in to help that old woman with her burst pipe this morning?' said Mr Tweeky. 'Well, I took my coat and hat off and hung them in the hall. When I came downstairs to put them on again, I must have put on someone else's red coat. And that's why all those lovely things were in the pockets!'

'Then the sausage and jam roll weren't magic!' said Higgle. 'They were someone else's.'

'Yes,' said Mr Tweeky mournfully. 'And I've eaten them. And we've eaten all the sweets. And there's jam all over the handkerchief. And I've spent some of the money. Whatever shall I do?'

'You'll have to go back and own up,' said Higgle sorrowfully. 'I'm ever so sorry for you, Tweeky; I really *did* think you'd got a bit of good luck today – and it's turned out to be *bad* luck after all!'

Mr Tweeky stopped the bus and got down. Higgle jumped down too.

'I'll come back with you,' he said comfortingly. 'I'll tell the old woman that you thought it was magic and didn't know you were eating anyone else's dinner.'

So the two friends walked all the way back to the old woman's house. It was evening when they reached there, and when at last they stood outside the house, they heard a voice talking loudly inside one of the front rooms.

'Come on, we must go in and tell Mr Hubble-Bubble what you've done,' whispered Higgle. So the two went up the path and knocked at the front door.

'My lovely dinner had changed into dry bread!' said the voice. 'And my toffees were gone! I hadn't got my pencils or my fountain pen, and even my new gloves and nice silk handkerchiefs had disappeared. Someone must have put a bad spell on me, that's what *I* think! Oh, dear me, how horrid it is! I really do feel most unhappy!'

The old woman came to open it and bade Tweeky and Higgle come inside out of the cold. They followed her into a cosy room where a little old man, just as round as Tweeky, was walking up and down.

'Please,' said Mr Tweeky in a small voice, 'I've come to say that owing to a mistake, and our coats being so much alike, I took yours this morning and left my own.'

'Bless us all!' cried the little old man in joy. 'Then there isn't a spell on me after all! It was *your* dinner I found, and *your* red handkerchief I used! Well, well, well!'

'I'm sorry to say that I thought I had some magic about me,' said Mr Tweeky. 'So I decided your dinner was mine changed into something better. And I'm also sorry to say that I've eaten your sweets and spent some of your money, and made your blue handkerchief jammy.'

The little old lady began to laugh. Then Mr Hubble-Bubble began to smile too, and soon he was chuckling loudly.

'This is very funny,' he said. 'Very funny indeed.'

'*I* don't think it is,' said poor Mr Tweeky. 'I can't pay you back for your dinner or sweets, because I've only got twopence in the world, and I'm out of work.'

'Then it isn't funny at all,' said the old man, looking grave. 'But, tell me, how did you get my coat?'

Mr Tweeky told him.

'Oh, so you're the kind person who came and helped my wife this morning,' said the old man. 'Well, now, I need a really good, hard-working gardener, someone who will look after my wife as well when things go wrong in the house. Would you like the job?'

Mr Tweeky could hardly speak for joy. It was just the sort of work he loved. Higgle spoke up for his friend, and said what a kind, helpful fellow he was; so the old man engaged him on the spot.

'So it *was* my lucky day, after all!' said Mr Tweeky, as he struggled into his old coat and gave up the one he had been wearing. 'I'm very happy again now.'

And off he marched with Higgle, both of them as merry as blackbirds!

Lambs' Tails

Lambs' Tails

A Tale of the Big Bad Wolf

ONCE UPON a time there was a wicked enchanter who had been turned into a pure white wolf. He roamed about the world eating little pigs and big pigs, hens and ducks and anything else he could find. He was a big bad wolf and everyone knew about him.

The little lambs in the field had been warned about him. 'Don't speak to any strange animal you see,' said the mother sheep. 'Don't listen to any tales he tells. It might be the big bad wolf who is talking to you!'

Now there were some little lambs who thought

themselves very clever, and they longed to see more of the world than their own small green field. So one day, when two lambs found a little gap in the hedge, they called the others and one by one the foolish little creatures squeezed through it and found themselves out on the wide hillside, all alone. How excited they were! You should have seen them leap about, wriggle their long tails, and cry 'Maa-aa!' in excitement.

The mother sheep heard them, and ran to the gap in the hedge. 'Baa-aa! Come back!' they cried. But the lambs laughed and ran off. The sheep were too big to get through the gap, and they stood round and baa-aaed loudly and sorrowfully. The magical brownies that lived in the old hollow tree heard them and came to see what was the matter. When they heard what had happened they set off to find the foolish lambs.

The lambs had scampered far away over the hill and down the other side – and who should they meet but the big bad wolf! How his eyes gleamed when he saw the lambs.

'Good morning, pretty young creatures!' he cried. 'Come with me and I will show you where the sweetest, juiciest grass in the world grows!'

The little lambs followed him happily, and he took them into a thick hazel wood, meaning to make them invisible, pop them into his sack and take them home to eat for a whole week's dinners. He told the lambs to stand round him, and then he began to mutter the spell that would make them disappear.

But alas for him! He couldn't make their little wriggling tails disappear! All the rest of the lambs' woolly bodies vanished – but their frisky tails stayed there, whisking about in a ridiculous manner.

'Bother!' said the wolf, and took a pair of scissors from his pocket. Snip! Snip! Snip! He cut off each tail and packed the frightened lambs into his sack. Then he gathered up the snipped-off tails and threw them over his shoulder into the bare twigs of the hazel tree

39

behind them. They stuck there and grew. The wolf shouldered his sack and ran off through the wood, chuckling to think that no one would ever find out what he had done.

But the brownies saw those curious lambs' tails on the hazel twigs and were surprised to see how they wriggled and shook, just as if they were alive. 'They are the lambs' tails,' cried the brownies, 'and see – here are the tracks of the big bad wolf!' After him they went and caught him easily. He dropped his sack and fled away.

The lambs were soon made to appear again by the brownies and went back to their field, sad and sorry, without any tails at all. And ever since that day the hazel trees have grown wriggling lambs' tails that dance and shake in the wind as if they were alive. Have you seen them?

The Little Bear's Adventure

The Little Bear's Adventure

ONCE UPON a time there was a little brown bear. He lived on the top shelf in the toyshop, with his best friend, a duck. They had been there for a whole year. Fancy that! A whole year!

They were very unhappy about it. They got dustier and dustier, and had almost given up hope of ever being sold. They longed to have a little boy or girl to own them.

You see, by some mistake, the duck had a bear's growl and the bear had a duck's quack. It was most upsetting. Whenever the bear was squeezed in his middle, he said 'Quack!' very loudly indeed – and whenever the duck was squeezed she said 'Grr-rrr!'

The shopkeeper had tried to sell them, but she couldn't, and so she had put them away on the top shelf.

One day a little girl came into the shop with her mother. She had come to spend the money that her granny had given her for her birthday.

'I want a bear and a duck,' she said. Then she pointed up to the shelf. 'Oh, look!' she said. 'There's a lovely little brown bear, and he has a duck right next to him.'

The shopkeeper took them down – how excited the bear and duck felt when they thought they might be sold to this nice little girl!

'Do they say anything?' she asked.

'Well,' said the shopkeeper, 'it's rather funny. The bear quacks like a duck, and the duck growls like a bear. A mistake was made and it is impossible to put it right.'

The little girl pressed the bear and he made a loud

quack. Then she pressed the duck and of course she had to growl – 'Grr-rrr!'

'Oh,' said the little girl, disappointed, 'what a pity! They make the wrong sounds. I'm afraid I don't want them.'

The little bear was quite upset. He put a comforting paw on Duck's shoulder. The little girl looked at them again, and they looked so sad that she felt quite sorry for them.

'I'd like to get a bear that growls properly and a duck that quacks in the right way,' she said. 'But if I can't I might come back and buy these two.'

'Very well,' said the shopkeeper, and she put the two toys back on the top shelf again. They watched the little girl go out of the shop. They felt most unhappy. To think they could have gone to live with a nice girl like that.

That night the bear spoke to the duck. 'Quack!' he said. 'Duck, listen to me. It's quite time we did something to help ourselves.'

'Grr-rrr!' said the duck.

'We will go to the wise woman on the hill,' said the bear, 'and ask for her help. Maybe she can do something for us.' He jumped down from the shelf, went over to a window which was open at the bottom, and jumped through.

'Come on, Duck,' he called, and the duck waddled out behind him across the wet grass.

After a long walk, they came to the hill where the wise woman lived. Her cottage was at the top, and the two toys could see that it was brightly lit.

The wise woman was having a party, but just as the two toys approached, the guests began to leave. Out went Dame Big-Feet the witch, on her broomstick. Out went Mrs Twinkle, the plump, jolly woman who sold balloons, and Mr Poker-Man, who was as tall and as thin as a poker. Last of all went Roll-Around, who was as round as a ball and rolled along instead of walking.

The two toys hid outside until all the goodbyes

were said, and then they crept out. They peered in at the window, and to their great surprise they saw the wise woman sitting on a chair, groaning and crying.

'Oh my!' she said. 'I'm so tired and there's all this mess to clear up before I go to bed.'

The bear felt sorry for the unhappy little woman. He knocked on the door and went in.

'We will clear up everything for you,' he said. 'Don't worry. My friend Duck will make you a nice cup of tea and a hot-water bottle, and I will sweep up the mess, clear the table and wash up.'

The wise woman was so surprised that she didn't know what to say.

'Where have you two come from?' she asked at last. 'And why have you come to visit me tonight?'

'Never mind,' said the bear, deciding not to talk about his own troubles now. 'Why don't you snuggle into bed. Leave the rest to us.'

'Grr-rrr!' growled the duck kindly, much to the wise woman's surprise.

'Quack!' said the bear, and surprised her still more. Then she remembered that her friend, the toyshop woman, had told her about a bear who quacked and a duck who growled, and she thought these must be the two strange toys. How kind they were to come and look after her like this, just when she had so much clearing up to do!

Before the wise woman went to get ready for bed, the duck made her a nice cup of tea and gave her a hot-water bottle.

The bear was very busy too. He cleared all the dirty dishes, washed them up, put them neatly away and swept the floor. Then he put the cakes into their tins and the biscuits into their jars, and put the lids on.

He was very hungry, but of course he didn't dream of taking even half a biscuit. He knew it would be wrong and he was a very good little bear.

'She's almost asleep,' said the duck, peeking round the bedroom door. 'We'd better go.'

'I'm not quite asleep,' said the wise woman in a drowsy voice. 'Before you go, look in my kitchen drawer. You will find two boxes of pills there. Bear, take a yellow pill, Duck, take a blue one. You won't be sorry you came to help me tonight.'

'Thank you,' said the bear, astonished.

He knew that the wise woman had many marvellous spells and he wondered what would happen when he and the duck swallowed the pills.

Perhaps he would grow beautiful whiskers and maybe the duck would grow a wonderful tail.

He took a yellow pill and the duck swallowed a blue one. Then they carefully shut the kitchen drawer, called goodnight to the wise woman and went out into the night.

They were very tired when they got back to the toyshop. They climbed up to their shelf, leant back against the wall and fell fast asleep at once.

They didn't wake up until the sun was shining into the shop. The doorbell woke them with a jump and they sat up. They saw the same little girl who had come to the shop the day before. She looked up at their shelf and pointed to them.

'I've come back to see that bear and duck again,' she said.

The shopkeeper lifted them down. 'It is a pity the duck growls and the bear quacks,' she said.

She pressed the duck in the middle – and to everyone's enormous surprise the duck said 'Quack!' very loudly. The most surprised of all was the duck herself. She had never in her life said 'Quack!' and it felt very funny indeed.

Then the little girl squeezed the bear and to his delight he growled!

'Grr-rrr!' he went. Just like that.

'What a funny thing,' said the little girl. 'Have you had them mended?'

'No,' said the shopkeeper, just as surprised as the little girl. 'They've not been taken down from their shelf since you went out of the shop. I can't think what has happened to them.'

The little girl pressed the bear and the duck again. 'Grr-rrr!' growled the bear. 'Quack!' said the duck. They were both most delighted. So that was what the pills from the wise woman had done – given them the right voices!

'Well, I will buy them,' said the little girl. 'They are just what I wanted. I think the bear is lovely and the duck is a dear. I shall love them very much.'

How pleased the two toys were when they heard that! When the shopkeeper popped them into a box they hugged one another hard – so hard that the duck had to say 'Quack!' and the bear had to say 'Grr-rrr!'

'Listen to that!' said the little girl, laughing. 'They're saying that they're glad to come home with me.'

The Dumpy-Witch's Garden

The Dumpy-Witch's Garden

ONCE UPON a time the Dumpy-Witch came to live in Fairyland. Everyone was sorry, for the fairies hate witches. But the Dumpy-Witch only laughed when she heard that the fairies didn't want her. She had come to Fairyland and there she meant to stay.

She took a little crooked cottage on a hilltop. Around it lay a garden. The pixie who had lived there before had kept the garden really beautiful. There were rose trees there and big bushes of lavender. There were nasturtiums climbing up the wall and a great big patch of sunflowers in one corner.

The witch hated flowers. She didn't want a single

one in her garden. So she called in Snoopy, the old gardener who lived at the bottom of the hill, and told him to dig up all the plants.

'What, dig up all the flowers?' cried Snoopy in horror. 'Don't you want a garden then? Everyone in Fairyland has a garden and keeps it beautiful.'

'Do as I tell you,' snapped the Dumpy-Witch, looking at Snoopy out of her deep, green eyes so that he trembled and shook. 'Dig up everything! Burn it on a rubbish heap! And then get some big square flagstones, fit them together and pave the garden from end to end so that nothing can grow there!'

Snoopy set to work. He brought his spade and dug up everything – but he didn't burn it. No, he wheeled all the plants down the hill to his own garden and with loving hands he planted the rose trees there and everything else too. Then he bought some flagstones and carefully laid them together in the witch's garden so that it was just nothing but a paved stone yard, cold and ugly. The witch looked at it and was pleased.

'Ha!' she said. 'No flowers can grow there now! Mine will be the only garden in Fairyland without flowers. How annoyed the fairies will be!'

Snoopy looked at the witch and a funny little smile came over his tanned face. The Dumpy-Witch saw it.

'What are you smiling at?' she demanded fiercely. 'Tell me, quickly, or I'll turn you into a ladybird!'

'There are worse things than ladybirds!' said Snoopy. 'But I'll tell you what I was smiling at, Dumpy-Witch. I was smiling because you thought you wouldn't get flowers in this ugly stone yard. You will! Yes, you will! You can't stop them coming!'

The Dumpy-Witch frowned.

'You don't know what you are talking about!' she said. 'I shall put a spell along all the walls so that no one can get near enough to plant a single seed in the yard – not that anything would grow in such a stony place anyhow! And if no one can get in to plant seeds, no flowers will grow!'

But still old Snoopy smiled away and he shook his

grey head at the angry witch.

'You may think you're powerful with your big spells, Dumpy-Witch,' he said. 'But there's someone more powerful than you in Fairyland. Wait and see!'

'Well, if there's anyone more powerful than I am in Fairyland, I'll go as soon as I find it's true!' said the witch sharply. 'Now get away from here and don't come back.'

Snoopy went down the hill, still smiling. The witch went into her crooked cottage and took out her magic books. She hunted through them till she found the spell she wanted to set round the garden walls, to prevent anyone from coming near.

'There!' she said. 'Now not a single plant can spring up, for no one can get near to sow seeds!'

After that she shut herself up in the sitting room with a fire that burned blue flames, and began to study deep magic for weeks and weeks on end. She didn't know if the sun was shining, she didn't know when it was raining – she just sat and thought of spells and magic, enchantments and bewitchments.

Outside the sun shone, the rain rained and the wind blew. Yes, the wind blew. It peeped into that ugly paved garden and it didn't like what it saw there.

'Shocking!' said the wind. 'Fancy a garden like that in Fairyland! Really shocking!'

Then the wind went out hunting. How it hunted! It hunted for dandelion clocks and blew the fluffy seeds into the air. It hunted for daisy seeds and thistle seeds. It looked for the tall, pink willow-herb and blew handfuls of its seeds away into the air. It went wandering into the trees, and took some ash keys and sycamore keys spinning round and round through the autumn air. It found some yellow groundsel and blew the fluffy seeds away. Oh, I couldn't tell you *how* many seeds it found.

It blew most of them over the garden wall belonging to the Dumpy-Witch. No spell could keep the wind away – it was stronger than any magic in the world. The fluffy seeds flew merrily over the wall and settled down in the cracks between the rows of paving stones. They settled in the crevices of the wall, and one bold seed even found a landing place in the crack of the sitting room windowsill. Oh, there were plenty of seeds planted in that ugly garden before the winter was out!

In the springtime the seeds sprouted and grew. Little green leaves shot up everywhere, in between the paving stones. The garden was warm and sheltered and the small plants grew splendidly. The seed that had planted itself in the windowsill crevice was a sturdy daisy, and it sent up dozens of fat, green buds. They opened into white-petalled flowers with golden hearts, and knocked softly against the windowpane.

The Dumpy-Witch heard the strange noise and looked up with a frown. When she saw the pretty flowers growing outside she dropped her book in amazement. She ran to the window – and dear me, what a mass of flowers met her eye! Groundsel, daisies, dandelions – willow-herbs springing up ready to flower later, thistles in bud, their splendid prickly leaves standing sturdily out from their stem – and actually two small trees, one a sycamore and one an ash, growing twig-like out of the crack between two paving stones near the bottom of the garden!

The Dumpy-Witch gave a mournful cry and clapped her hands to her head.

'Who has done it?' she cried. 'Someone has been into my garden and planted seeds! Someone is more powerful than my magic! Who is it? Who is it?'

She sent for Snoopy again and showed him her flowery garden.

'Someone has been here and planted seeds,' she said. 'I am afraid. If it is someone very powerful they may come and take me prisoner, for I have many enemies. Do you know who it is, Snoopy?'

Snoopy looked round the garden with a wise eye. He knew perfectly well that the wind plants seeds everywhere. He looked at the trembling witch and shook his head sternly.

'Dumpy-Witch, Dumpy-Witch,' he said very slowly and solemnly, 'someone more powerful than all the witches together has been here. I can hear him coming now! Now! NOW! Get your broomstick and fly away before he gets you! He has planted your garden in spite of your spells . . . listen, listen – here he comes!'

The wind stirred outside the garden, and the witch thought it was some great enemy hiding there. With a scream of fright she caught up her broomstick, leapt on the handle and sailed high into the air. Nobody ever saw her again.

'Good riddance!' said old Snoopy, staring at the little black speck disappearing in the sky. 'She may be clever – but she isn't wise enough to know the ways of the wind!'

He set to work to dig up the ugly paving stones, and soon he had dug over the garden and made it ready to be planted properly. He had neat little packets of seeds all ready – nasturtiums, candytuft, marigolds and a hundred others.

'You're all right for planting weeds, old wind!' said Snoopy. 'But *I'm* going to plant the garden *this* time!'

The wind laughed – and when Snoopy had done it blew a handful of dandelion clocks over the wall. It meant to plant what it pleased too!

You'd Better Be Careful, Stamp-About!

You'd Better Be Careful, Stamp-About!

IT ALL began one morning when Mr Stamp-About took a walk down Bramble Lane. He wasn't in a very good temper because his egg had been bad at breakfast time, and he stamped along, frowning and grumbling to himself.

'I don't know what hens are coming to! Laying bad eggs! And to think I took such a big spoonful too! Ugh!'

He came to Dame Kindly's cottage and as he passed by her hedge, a spray of wild rose swung in the wind and scratched his cheek. Mr Stamp-About was very angry indeed.

'What! You'd lash out at me and scratch me like a cat!' he shouted, and he hit out at the wild rose bush with his stick. But the rose bush only swung back again and scratched his ear.

Mr Stamp-About marched into the little garden and glared at the bush, which was covered with lovely roses. He saw a spade lying not far off and snatched it up. In no time he had dug up the wild rose bush.

'There! That'll teach you to scratch people coming down the lane!' he shouted, and he stamped on the rose bush, which was now lying on the ground.

Dame Kindly couldn't believe her eyes when she looked out of her window. She knocked loudly on the pane. 'What are you doing? How dare you?'

Then Mr Stamp-About caught sight of three plump hens pecking about nearby, and he roared at them. 'Are you hens laying bad eggs? Was it one of you who laid the egg I had for breakfast? Well, let me tell you I won't put up with it! Shoo! Go into your hen house and sit down and lay good eggs. Shoo!'

And he waved his stick at the frightened hens and sent them scurrying away in fright. One fled out of the garden gate, squawking, and Dame Kindly came hurrying out of her door.

'Stop that! Stamp-About, how dare you chase my hens? Now one has fled away and I don't expect I'll ever get her back. And just look at my favourite wild rose bush!'

'Pah! You've no right to have a bush that lashes out and scratches people,' said Mr Stamp-About most unreasonably. 'As for the hens, I was only telling yours what I think about birds that lay bad eggs. I had one for breakfast, and it tasted so—'

'Stamp-About, get out of my garden and stop talking silly nonsense!' said Dame Kindly. 'If you don't, I'll tell my husband to come and chase you out just as you chased my hens!'

Stamp-About gave such a loud laugh that the cat nearby fled away and hid in fright. 'What! Tell your husband to chase me? That silly little man, who hardly comes up to my waist? You tell him I'll come and give him one good shove – and down he'll go, bump!'

Then out of the gate he went and gave it such a slam that the latch broke at once. Dame Kindly stared after him with angry tears in her eyes. To think that anyone should speak to her like that!

Someone called to her over the fence. It was little Long-Beard the brownie.

'Don't you take any notice of him, Dame Kindly. He's a loud-voiced bully. Just you send him in a bill for a new rose bush, and if your hen doesn't come back, tell him to pay for a new one. You get your husband to do that for you!'

'I will!' said Dame Kindly. So when her husband came home from work she told him all about Stamp-About's doings. The little man listened and frowned.

'Oh dear! I wish I was a great big fellow and could go after him! But he's so enormous and I'm so small, and he knows it. Still – I'll certainly send him in a bill if our hen doesn't come back.'

So when the hen didn't appear that day or the next, he made out a bill.

To Mr Stamp-About.
Bill for:
One rose bush,
    pulled up in a temper   £2
One hen,
    driven away in a temper   £5
One gate latch,
    broken in a temper   £3
Upsetting my wife   £10
                         £20

Payable to Mr Kindly AT ONCE.

Well, when Stamp-About got this bill he couldn't believe his eyes. Good gracious, what a temper he flew into! He stamped about his kitchen, shouting and yelling, till his next-door neighbour wondered if he had gone mad. He came peeping in at the window to see.

Stamp-About saw him and called him in. 'Hey, Mr Snoopy, come and see the bill that Mr Kindly has had the cheek to send in to me. What would you do if he had sent it to you?'

'Oh,' said Snoopy slyly. 'I'd fight him, Mr Stamp-About. Biff, like this! Smash, like that!' And he hit out at the air in front of him gleefully. 'Down he'd go – and you could demand money from him then for insulting you by sending in such a rude bill!'

'That's a good idea of yours,' said Stamp-About. 'A very, very good idea. I'll send him a letter to say I'll be along tomorrow morning at ten o'clock to fight. Aha! He's such a tiny fellow, I can shake him to bits if I want to and then throw him into his duck pond!'

So he wrote a letter to Mr Kindly and sent Mr Snoopy with it. Mrs Kindly opened it, because her husband was at work, and she sobbed bitterly when she read it.

'How unkind! What would my husband do against a man like Stamp-About? I've a good mind to go and buy a grow-big spell from Witch Long-Nose, and make my husband drink it. Then he could defeat Stamp-About – and serve him right!'

Snoopy hurried back to tell Stamp-About this. 'Oh – so she thinks she can play a trick like that on me, does she?' he shouted. 'Well – I'll be there at nine o'clock, instead of ten, before he's drunk any spell at all.'

Now it happened that Snoopy met Long-Beard the brownie that morning, and he told him how Stamp-About was going to fight little Mr Kindly – and that he was going to be at his house at nine o'clock, instead of ten, so that Mr Kindly wouldn't have had time to drink the grow-big spell. He laughed and laughed as he told Long-Beard about it, for Snoopy was not a nice fellow at all – but Long-Beard was worried. He didn't want the nice, friendly Kindlys to be upset and hurt.

He hurried off to Witch Long-Nose, and out of his own money he bought two bottles of spells. One was labelled DRINK THIS AND GROW LITTLE and one was labelled DRINK THIS AND GROW BIG.

Long-Beard went to Mr and Mrs Kindly's cottage and knocked at the door. Soon he was telling them that Stamp-About meant to come at nine o'clock instead of ten, hoping that Mr Kindly hadn't yet drunk the spell.

'But now listen,' said Long-Beard. 'Don't drink the grow-big spell, Mr Kindly. It tastes horrible, and growing big is very painful, and you would look dreadful, and—'

'Well, I'm certainly not going to drink the grow-little spell!' said Kindly.

'I know. Watch what I'm going to do,' said Long-Beard. He carefully took off the two labels from the bottles and stuck them on again – but on the wrong bottles!

'Now listen!' he said, as he pressed the grow-little

label on to the bottle of grow-big. 'At nine o'clock tomorrow morning, you and Mrs Kindly must come and hide in my house – but leave these bottles on the table. If I know anything of Stamp-About, as soon as he sees it he'll drink the grow-big spell – or what he thinks is the grow-big spell – and then, to his enormous surprise, he'll find himself dwindling away to the size of your cat!'

Mr Kindly roared with laughter. 'Long-Beard, you're too clever for words!' he said. 'Right. We'll do what you say.'

So just before nine o'clock the next morning the two Kindlys went into Long-Beard's cottage and hid there, peeping out behind the curtain to watch for Stamp-About. On their kitchen table they had left the two bottles – the grow-big spell labelled GROW LITTLE and the grow-little spell labelled GROW BIG.

'And if old Stamp-About likes to steal one of them by drinking it, he's only got himself to blame!' chuckled Long-Beard.

Well, at exactly nine o'clock, along came Stamp-About, singing a rude song about Mr Kindly and swinging a stout stick. He thundered on the front door, but nobody came.

So he went round to the back door and looked in at the kitchen window. Ha – what were those two bottles standing on the table? He pushed open the back door and went in to see.

'What! A grow-big spell! So old Kindly got one after all and meant to drink it before I came! And a grow-little spell to force down my throat when he had defeated me because he had grown so big. Ha – he's made a very big mistake! I'll drink the grow-big spell!'

And with that he took out the cork, tipped up the bottle and drank the whole spell down! Gulp-swallow-gulp!

But, of course, it was the grow-little spell he had drunk! Stamp-About, who had been expecting to grow big and touch the ceiling, found himself growing

76

small. Smaller – smaller – smaller still! Whatever was happening?

He gave a howl of fright. Why, he was smaller than the table – his head didn't even reach the top! Now he was so small that he wouldn't be able even to sit on the stool!

Next door Mr and Mrs Kindly and Long-Beard were waiting to see what happened. All they heard was a small frightened howling, rather like a puppy whining.

'He's drunk it – he's drunk the grow-little spell, thinking it was the grow-big spell, just as we hoped!' said Kindly. 'Come along – we'll go and see!'

Yes – he was right, of course. How the Kindlys and Long-Beard laughed to see such a very small Stamp-About, howling in fright, trying his best to climb up on to a chair.

'Well, little fellow – what about that fight with me?' said Mr Kindly.

'No! No, no, no!' whimpered Stamp-About, trying

to hide under the stool. 'Don't be a bully!'

Then who should come into the kitchen but Whiskers, Mrs Kindly's cat. As soon as she saw the tiny little Stamp-About she hissed – and sprang! Stamp-About was so scared that he ran straight out of the door. The cat went after him. How it chased him – first into this corner, and then into that. What a dreadful time poor Stamp-About had!

'It'll eat me! Save me, save me!' he cried.

Mrs Kindly began to feel very sorry for him. 'Hasn't he been punished enough?' she said.

'No,' said Long-Beard. 'Let him be chased for five minutes more! Then maybe he'll talk some sense.'

So for another five minutes the tiny Stamp-About was pounced on, and chased here and there – and then Kindly picked him up and looked at him.

'Listen,' he said. 'I'm not going to fight you – I left my cat to do that. But what about that bill of mine? Are you going to pay for that rose bush and my hen?'

'Yes, oh, yes,' wept Stamp-About. 'Only let me go,

I must get a grow-big spell from somewhere.'

'Well, drink a bit out of this grow-little bottle,' said Kindly. 'We changed the labels. This is the spell to make you grow big! But don't you forget to pay our bill, Stamp-About – or we'll tell everyone in the village how our cat chased you round our garden, and they'll laugh whenever they meet you.'

'No – don't tell them, please don't,' begged Stamp-About. 'Let me have a drink of that other spell. I hope it's not as painful as this one is!'

He drank some of the spell that would make him grow big again – and suddenly shot up to his right size. He sat down in a chair and groaned.

'I feel peculiar. My head is spinning. Take me home!'

'I'll take him home,' said Long-Beard. 'But first of all, what about the money for that bill of Kindly's, Stamp-About?'

'Take it out of my pocket,' groaned Stamp-About. 'Take all you want. I feel ill. I want to go home.

All these spells – they don't suit me!'

So Long-Beard took the money from Stamp-About's pocket and gave it to Mr Kindly to pay his bill. Then he pulled him to his feet to take him home.

'You've had a jolly good lesson, Stamp-About,' he said. 'You behave yourself in future.'

Well, I don't expect old Stamp-About really will alter his ways – but I do know this: whenever he passes the Kindlys' cottage, he runs like a hare if he sees their cat on the wall. And I'm not a bit surprised at that, are you?

The Spell That Went Wrong

The Spell That Went Wrong

THERE WAS once a very clever brownie called Big-Head, who could make wonderful magic spells.

He had a little goblin servant called Heyho. Heyho had to run about and get Big-Head the things he needed for his spells.

One day Little-One the red imp came to see Big-Head. Little-One was not a nice imp at all. He was spiteful and mean, and nobody liked him. But he was very, very rich. No one knew how many sacks of gold he had, for he kept them locked up in a cave, deep in the heart of a hill.

'What do you want, Little-One?' asked the clever

brownie. 'Is there anything you want me to sell you? I have some marvellous spells.'

'Big-Head, I want to be strong and big,' said Little-One the imp. 'I am tired of being small. I want to grow as big as a hill, as strong as an oak tree, as mighty as the wind that roars in wintertime. I will pay you well if you can get me a spell that will make me big.'

'Little-One, I don't think you are good enough to be made strong and powerful,' said Big-Head. 'You see, only really good and wise people should be given strength and power, for if wicked people are strong, then they can make others very unhappy.'

'I shall be very, very good and wise when I am big and powerful,' said Little-One. 'I am only mean and spiteful because I am small and people laugh at me. But as soon as I am tall and strong, you will see what good things I do! I shall be the finest imp that ever lived.'

'Will you really?' said Big-Head. 'Well, it would

be worth making you big then. But you are quite sure, Little-One, that you will use your strength and power well, and not ill, if I give you a spell to make you big?'

'I promise,' said Little-One. But he did not mean it. He only wanted to be big and strong so that he might get richer still, so that he might punish the people he did not like and make everyone fear him.

But Big-Head the brownie believed him. He called his servant Heyho to him and told him about the imp.

'Little-One wants to be made big and strong and powerful,' he said. 'He will give me as much gold as I like if I give him the spell he wants.'

'What things do you want for your spell?' asked Heyho. Big-Head had to think about that. It would be a difficult spell to make, he knew. But at last, by thinking and dreaming hard, he knew how to make the spell for Little-One.

'*Fruit of the oak, keys of the ash,*
Rumble of thunder, and lightning-flash,

Thread of a spider, wing of a bee,
Breath from the gale blowing over the sea,
Tooth of a lion, a limpet's shell –
These are the things that I need for my spell!'

This was the spell song that Heyho heard his master singing. He sighed. What a lot of things to find for the spell! Well, Big-Head would have to wait for some of them. It was only springtime now, and the oak and the ash were hardly in leaf, and the fruit would not be ready till the autumn.

Big-Head knew what Heyho was thinking.

'You can find me nearly all the things quickly, but I must wait for the fruit of the oak and the ash,' he said. 'Choose a big oak tree, the biggest you can find, Heyho, and a big ash tree, and watch the flower carefully, so that you may choose me the finest, strongest fruit from the trees in the autumn. Get me the other things as soon as you can and store them in the big blue pan for me.'

So Heyho got all the other things, and he was really very clever at getting them, for it is not easy to get a rumble of thunder and a flash of lightning.

Still, he managed it, and put them into the big blue pan. The thunder kept rumbling round the pan and made a noise, but nobody minded.

It was easy to get a strong silken thread from a spider's web and the strong little wing from a dead bee. Heyho got the tooth of a lion quite easily, because he looked for a lion with toothache, and took out the bad tooth. It was enormous.

'Now, a limpet's shell,' said Heyho. 'I must go to the sea for that, and for the breath of a gale too. Let me see now – the limpet has a shell like a pointed hat, and it is very, very strong.'

He found an empty limpet shell, and then he caught a breath from the rough gale and put it into a bottle to take home and empty into the blue pan.

Now he only had the fruit of the oak and the ash to take, and then Big-Head could stir everything up together and say the magic words to make the spell.

'All the same, I wish he wasn't going to give the spell to that nasty Little-One,' said Heyho. 'I know he will use his power badly.'

Heyho went out to find an oak tree and an ash tree. He knew them both. They were immensely strong trees, tall and beautiful. They were just beginning to leaf.

Heyho chose a great oak tree. It was putting out tender reddish-green leaves. Among the leaves Heyho found the flowers. There were two kinds, both catkins.

One was a small, thin catkin, with bunches of yellow-headed stamens growing on it. The other was a stouter, upright catkin, set with two or three tiny cups. In the middle of each cup was a seed-vessel.

'I'll watch you carefully,' said Heyho. 'I'll choose your finest fruit, oak tree.'

Then he went to the ash tree, whose black buds had broken out into thousands of peculiar little flowers, that opened before the leaves unfolded. There were bunches of purple stamens in the midst of which stood little bottle-shaped seed-vessels of green.

Heyho looked at the flowers. 'I shall watch you changing into ash keys,' he said. 'Ash keys are your fruit, ash tree. I shall pick them when they are green, before the "spinners" come whirling down to the ground!'

The ash tree put out its leaves when the flowers had faded and were already beginning to form into ash keys. They were beautiful feathery leaves, light and strong, cut into pale-green leaflets.

Soon the oak too, was covered in feather-shaped leaves, and its stamen catkins had faded and withered. But the little cup-like seed-vessels were growing well.

Heyho forgot to watch the oak and the ash trees. He didn't notice how the fruits were growing. He just didn't bother. But Big-Head gave him a shock one day.

'Heyho! I want to make that spell for Little-One tomorrow. He is coming to me with twenty sacks of gold. Have you everything I need for the spell?'

'Oh, good gracious!' said Heyho. 'Yes – no – yes – er – I mean no, not quite. There's everything there except the fruit of the ash or oak.'

'Go and get them at once,' said Big-Head crossly. 'It is autumn, and they should be ready.'

Heyho rushed off. He plucked some of the ash keys, which were now big and well formed. Then he ran to the oak. He saw a good many little round brown balls growing on the twigs and he picked some quickly. Then he hurried back and put the ash keys and the round brown balls into the blue pan.

'Ready, master, ready,' he cried. Big-Head came up with his magic spoon. He stirred the curious mixture, and he sang a magic song. Everything grew quiet and small and green in the pan. At last, at the bottom, there were two or three drops of a curious shining green liquid. Big-Head tipped it out into a golden cup.

'Here is the strongest spell in the world!' he said. 'It will make Little-One as tall as a hill, as strong as the sea, as powerful as the wind!'

Little-One drank the spell the next day and everyone waited to see him grow enormous. But he didn't. He stayed small – but he went a curious green colour. Yes, his face and hands, and even his hair, turned a pale green!

'Something went wrong with the spell!' groaned Big-Head. 'What could it have been?'

And suddenly Heyho knew. 'Oh, master, do forgive me!' he cried. 'I know what I did wrong. I took the wrong thing from the oak tree. I took oak apples instead of acorns! I forgot they were not the real fruit of the oak tree!'

'You foolish fellow!' said Big-Head angrily. 'Oak apples are made by insects! They pierce an oak twig, lay eggs there, and cause a round ball to grow, in which their eggs hatch! The grub eats the soft juicy ball that has formed.'

'I know, I know,' wept poor Heyho. 'And those balls grow hard and woody and brown, don't they, master? Look – here is one I didn't put into the pan.'

He showed Big-Head a hard round ball. Big-Head pointed to a hole in it. 'That is where the insect came out,' he said. 'Now you have spoilt my spell, and turned Little-One green, instead of making him big and powerful!'

'It's a good thing, master, it's a good thing!' cried Heyho suddenly. 'I know Little-One is bad. He would never be good. He would have used his power to make people unhappy, not happy! It's a good thing the spell went wrong!'

And, indeed, it was. If Heyho hadn't made that mistake, and put oak apples into the spell instead of acorns, the red imp would have become big and strong enough to rule all the little folk! Then goodness knows what might have happened!

The Goat, the Duck, the Goose and the Rooster

The Goat, the Duck, the Goose and the Rooster

ONCE UPON a time there was a rooster who was very tired of living with the hens in his yard, so he made up his mind to run away and find other friends. He set off one morning at dawn, and it wasn't long before he met a fine goose, walking along the lane.

'Good morning, goose,' said the rooster. 'Where are you off to?'

'I have lost my mistress, the goose-girl,' said the goose. 'I am seeking another mistress now.'

'Come with me,' said the rooster, ruffling out his beautiful tail-feathers. 'I am going to see the world.'

So the goose and the rooster walked on together.

Presently they came to a little white duck waddling along as fast as her two unsteady legs would carry her.

'Good morning, duck,' said the rooster. 'Where are you off to?'

'I have heard bad news this morning,' said the duck. 'The red hen told me that my master was going to eat me for his supper. So I ran away, but I don't know where to go to.'

'Come with us,' said the rooster, standing on his toes, and looking very grand. 'We are going to see the world.'

So the duck went with the goose and the rooster, and they all walked down the lane together till they came to the common.

On the common was a billy-goat, and he had slipped the rope that tied him to his post, and was gambolling about free.

'Good morning,' said the rooster. 'What are you going to do?'

'I don't know,' said the goat joyously. 'I am free

for the first time in my life – but I don't know where to go.'

'Come with us,' said the rooster, making the red comb on his head stand up very high. 'We are going to see the world.'

So the goat went with the goose, the duck and the rooster, and they all walked over the common together.

'What shall we do?' asked the goat.

'Shall we go to the town of Nottingham and stand by the roadside?' said the rooster. 'I have a fine voice and I could sing for pennies.'

'I could take round the hat,' said the duck.

'I could clap my wings in time to your song,' said the goose.

'And I could butt anyone who wouldn't give us a penny,' said the goat.

So off they set for the town of Nottingham. When they got there it was market day and there were many folk about. The four animals stood by the side of the road and the rooster began to sing.

> '*Cock-a-doodle-doo,*
>   *My baby's lost her shoe,*
> *It had a button blue,*
>   *What shall Baby do?*'

The goose beat time with her wings and the duck took round a hat for pennies. The goat stood by ready to butt anyone who would not give them anything.

But before the rooster had quite finished his song a burly farmer came up.

'What's all this?' he cried. 'Here are four creatures escaped from their pens. Catch them!'

Without waiting a moment the four animals fled away. Through the streets of Nottingham they went and found themselves on the hill outside the town.

'We were nearly caught!' said the goat. 'We must not go near a town again. Whatever shall we do?'

'We had better find a cave to live in,' said the rooster. 'See, there is one halfway up the hillside.'

'A witch lives there with her daughter,' said the duck.

'We will go and ask her if there is another cave near by,' said the goose. So off they all went. But when they got to the cave it was empty. No one was there. But there was a cupboard full of good things and the hungry creatures had a good meal. Then they settled down to sleep.

Now that night the old witch and her daughter returned to the cave. They were a wicked couple and the people of Nottingham had long tried to get rid of them. The witch stepped into the cave first and lit a candle – and the first thing she saw was the table, spread with the remains of the animals' meal.

'Someone has been here!' she cried and stamped her foot. She and her daughter ran out of the cave and went to a nearby tree to think what they should do. They were afraid that an enemy was in the cave.

'Daughter, you creep back and find out,' said the witch. 'I will prepare a spell so that if any man or woman is in the cave they cannot harm you. Go.'

Now when the witch had shouted and stamped her foot, the four animals had awakened in fright. The goat was lying near the entrance of the cave, the goose was by the cupboard, the duck was under the table and the rooster was on the back of a chair. They waited to see if anything further would happen – and they heard the witch's daughter coming back.

It's my mistress! thought the goat.

It's my master! thought the duck.

It's my mistress! thought the rooster.

It's the goose-girl, thought the goose. And all of them were frightened.

The witch's daughter came creeping in. She heard nothing at all. She went to the table and trod on one of the duck's feet underneath.

'Quack-quack, quack-quack!' squawked the duck in pain and dug his beak into the girl's leg. In a great fright she stumbled towards the cupboard and fell over the goose.

'*Ss-ss-ss-ss-sss!*' hissed the goose, and struck the witch's daughter with its great wings. Then it began to cackle loudly in fright. The girl was afraid and sat down in a chair trembling. But when she leant back in the darkness she almost pushed the rooster off the back of the chair and he put his claws into her hair in terror, crying, 'Cock-a-doodle-doo! Cock-a-doodle-doo!'

The witch's daughter could not bear it any longer. She fled to the entrance of the cave and fell right over the goat. He butted her so that she was sent rolling over and over down the hillside and only came to rest under the tree beside the witch.

'What is the matter?' cried the witch. 'Didn't my spell work?'

'Oh mother, oh mother,' said the daughter, weeping. 'The cave is full of powerful wizards. When I went in there was one under the table that cried, "Go back, go back!" And then he struck my leg. By the cupboard is a snake that hissed at me in a dreadful manner, and then came at me with its head. On the back of a chair sits another wizard who cried, "What a rogue are you! What a rogue are you!" and then nearly pulled my hair out of my head. But worst of all is a giant wizard lying near the entrance. He flung me down the hillside, and here I am.'

'What a dreadful thing!' said the witch, trembling. 'Our sins have found us out. We must stay here no longer. Come, let us away before dawn.'

They hurried off and no one ever heard of them again. As for the four animals, they soon fell asleep and slept peacefully till morning. When they awoke they looked round the cave and were pleased.

'We will live here together,' said the rooster. 'No one will disturb us, for they think that this is the witch's home. We shall be happy here.'

They settled down in peace together, and as far as I know, there they may be living still!

The Goblin
Looking Glass

The Goblin
Looking Glass

IT WAS a very wet day and Micky and Pam couldn't go out to play in the garden. They were cross about it because they wanted to dig in their sandpit. They stood at the window and grumbled.

'It's no use being cross, my dears,' said Nurse. 'Get your bricks or your books and amuse yourselves. I am going down to help Mummy to make a new dress for Pam, so be good while I am gone.'

Nurse took her workbasket and went downstairs. The children were left alone. They turned away from the window and stared round the nursery.

'I don't want to play with bricks,' said Micky. 'And

I'm tired of all my books. I wish something exciting would happen.'

'Nothing lovely *ever* happens!' sighed Pam. 'You read of such glorious adventures in books – but nothing ever *really* happens to children like us.'

'There isn't even anything very exciting in the nursery,' said Micky. 'We haven't a gramophone like Peter has. And we haven't a nice clockwork railway like Jack's. There's nothing nice in our nursery at all.'

'No, nothing – except the big looking glass,' said Pam, pointing to a full-length mirror hung on the wall. The children liked this very much because they could see all of themselves in it, from top to toe. Round the mirror was carved a most exciting pattern of fruits, flowers and tiny little goblin-like creatures peeping out from the flowers. It really was a lovely looking glass.

Pam and Micky liked to look into it and see their nursery reflected there, the other way round. Micky looked at the mirror on that wet, rainy morning, and an idea came into his head.

'I wonder if there is anything magic about that mirror,' he said, going over to it. 'You know, it's very, very old, Pam. Let's look carefully at all those little goblins carved round it and see if we think there's any magic about them.'

So the two children looked carefully at each goblin, and rubbed each one to see if anything happened. But nothing did. Micky was disappointed. He leant against the mirror and looked into it at the nursery reflected there.

And then he saw a most strange and curious thing. He saw standing in the mirror-nursery a little carved chair, just by the fireplace – but when he looked back into the real nursery there was no chair at all!

'Pam! Pam! Look here!' he cried excitedly. 'Look into the mirror. Do you see that funny carved chair, standing by the fireplace? Well, it's in the mirror, but it isn't in our nursery! What do you think of that!'

Pam looked. Sure enough, it was just as Micky had said. A small carved chair stood in the looking glass – but it wasn't in the real nursery at all. It was only in the looking glass. It was carved like the mirror itself, and seemed to match it perfectly. Whose was it? Who sat there? And why was it in the looking glass but not in the nursery itself?

'Pam, Pam! Something exciting has happened at last!' cried Micky. He pressed his face against the glass to try and see further into the mirror – and suddenly he gave a great cry of surprise and fell right through the mirror into the reflection beyond!

Pam stared in astonishment. There was Micky on the other side of the mirror, staring at her, too surprised to speak. Then she heard his voice, sounding rather far away.

'Pam! I'm the other side of the mirror! Take my hand and come too. We'll have a real adventure!'

Pam stretched out her hand and took Micky's. He gave her a pull and she passed right through the looking glass and stood beside Micky. They looked back at their nursery – and as they looked, they saw the door open and Nurse come in.

'Don't let her see us,' whispered Micky. 'It would spoil everything. Quick, hide!'

He ran out of the door in the mirror with Pam. They expected to find themselves on the broad, sunny landing that lay outside their own nursery door – but the looking glass house was different. Instead of a wide landing there was a narrow, dark passage. Micky stopped.

'This is funny,' he said. 'It's quite different from our house. I wonder where we really are, now.'

Pam felt a bit frightened and wanted to go back, but Micky wouldn't let her. No, this was an adventure, and he wanted to go on with it. 'There's nothing to be afraid of,' he said. 'I'll look after you.'

He took Pam along the dark passage and came at last to stairs going up and down. They were peculiar stairs, going in a spiral, and the children wondered whether to go up them or down them. They decided to go up them.

So up they went and came at last to a big grey door set with orange nails. They pushed it open and looked inside. And they saw a very strange sight!

A small goblin-like man, with funny, pointy ears, sat hunched up in a corner by a big fireplace, leaning over a large red book. Tears were running down his cheeks and made a big pool at his feet. The children stared at him in surprise.

'What's the matter?' asked Micky, at last. The goblin jumped so much with fright that his book nearly fell into the fire. He snatched it out and sat down again on his stool, holding his hand to his beating heart.

'Oh!' he said. 'Oh! What a fright you gave me! I thought you were Bom, the big goblin. How in the world did you get here?'

'Oh, never mind that,' said Micky. 'We are here that's all. What were you crying for?'

'Look at this book,' said the goblin, beginning to cry again. 'It's a book of recipes. I've got to make some special lemonade for Bom, and I can't read very well, so I just simply can't find out how to make it! There are such long words here – and Bom will stand me in a corner all night if I haven't got the lemonade ready when he comes back.'

'I'll read it for you!' said Micky. He took the book and read out loud.

'Enchanted Lemonade. To Make: Take the juice of the five best lemons that have grown in the moonlight. Take some yellow honey from the bumblebee that visits the nightshade on Friday evening. Take a spoonful of blue sugar. Stir with a kingfisher's feather. Say five enchanted words over the mixture.'

'Oh, thank you!' cried the small goblin, delighted. 'Now I know exactly what to do. Oh, you really are kind and clever. I'll make the lemonade at once!'

He took five strange-looking, silvery lemons from

a dish in a cupboard. Then he found a tiny flute in one of his pockets and blew on it. In a moment or two a very large bumblebee flew in at the open window. The goblin spoke to it in a curious humming voice, and the bee flew out. It came back in a few minutes with a small jar of yellow honey, which the goblin took from it with a smile. Then out flew the bee again.

Micky and Pam watched in amazement. The goblin shook some blue sugar from a bag into a silver spoon and mixed it with the juice of the lemons and the honey. Then he took a bright blue feather from a jar and stirred the mixture, muttering over it the strangest words that the children had ever heard.

'There! It's made!' said the goblin happily, putting the bowl of lemonade on the windowsill. 'Thanks to you, little boy! But, tell me – what are you doing here in Bom's house? Does he know you are here?'

'No,' said Micky. 'I didn't even know it was Bom's house. We came through the mirror in our nursery, and found everything quite different.'

'You came through the mirror!' cried the little goblin in fright. 'Oh, be careful then! It's years and years since anyone did that. It's a sort of trap, you know. Bom always hopes someone will fall through that magic mirror one day, and then he finds them and makes them his servants for a hundred years. They are allowed to go back then, but, of course, they are old and so they never want to. They always end up as goblins, like me.'

Micky and Pam listened in astonishment and dismay. They wanted an adventure, but not a horrid one.

'Where is Bom?' asked Micky. 'Perhaps we can get back to our nursery before he sees us.'

'I don't think you can,' said the goblin. 'I believe I can hear him coming now. Quick, take these – they may help you sometime or other. Go and hide behind that couch. Maybe Bom won't see you then.'

Micky took what the goblin pressed into his hand and then dragged Pam behind the couch. It was only just in time. The door opened and through it came a magnificent goblin, dressed in a cloak of pure gold and a tunic of silver with sapphire buttons. His hat, which he hadn't bothered to take off, had a wonderful curling feather in it, and his long, pointed ears stuck out below it.

'Ho, Tumpy!' said Bom in a loud voice. 'Have you made that lemonade? Where is it?'

Tumpy, the little goblin, ran to the windowsill and fetched the bowl of lemonade. To the children's surprise Bom raised it to his lips and drank it all in one gulp.

'That's good,' he said. 'Very good.' Then he stood and sniffed the air as if he could smell something.

'Tumpy,' he said in an angry voice. 'You have had visitors. Where are they?'

Tumpy was very frightened but he wasn't going to give the children away. He shook his head and, taking up a broom, began to sweep the floor. But Bom took him up in his big hand and shook him so hard that

Micky and Pam were sure they could hear his teeth rattling together.

Micky was not going to let anyone be hurt for him. So he stepped boldly out from behind the couch with Pam.

'Stop shaking Tumpy,' he said. 'We are not really his visitors. We didn't come to see him.'

Bom dropped Tumpy in surprise and stared at the two children.

'Did you come to see *me*, then?' he asked. 'Oh, perhaps you are the two children of the wizard Broody? He told me he was sending them out travelling, and that they might perhaps call and see me.'

'Perhaps we are and perhaps we aren't,' said Micky grandly. 'We shall not tell you our names.'

Bom looked at them sharply. 'Well, if you are, you can do two or three things for me,' he said. 'I've a silver canary that won't sing. If you are the wizard's children, you can easily make it sing for me. Then I've a sack of stones I can't turn into gold, no matter how I try. You can do that for me too. Then I've a candle that won't light. You must make it light for me. If you can do those things I shall know you are the wizard's children and you shall go in safety. But – if you cannot do them, then who will you be? Perhaps children that have come through the goblin mirror! Aha!'

Micky put on a bold face and hoped that Pam would try not to cry. He meant to go back to the mirror room as soon as he had a chance, and climb through the looking glass into his own nursery.

'I'll try to do what you want,' he said. 'Take us to the canary.'

Bom marched to the door, and the children went after him. Micky looked behind him at the little goblin Tumpy, and saw that he was pointing and signalling to him. Micky knew why. It was to remind him that Tumpy had given him something. He patted his pocket to show Tumpy he remembered, and then followed the big goblin down the curly stairs.

Bom took them to a little room. There was only one thing in it and that was a big golden cage with a silver canary in it. The little bird sat glumly on its perch and its bright eyes looked at Bom and the children when they came in.

'This is the canary,' said Bom. 'He won't sing. Let me see you make him open his mouth and trill sweetly.'

'Oh, no, we cannot let you see our magic,' said Micky, much to Pam's surprise. 'You must leave us alone and come back in half an hour. We cannot do magic with a goblin looking on.'

'Very well,' said Bom, and he left the room. Micky was delighted. He waited until the goblin was gone and then he ran to the door.

'We can easily escape before he comes back,' he whispered to Pam. But alas! The door was locked on the outside. The children were prisoners.

Pam began to cry, but Micky wasted no time. He felt in his pocket to see what the little goblin Tumpy had given him. He took the things out.

There was a red feather, very tiny. A shining golden button – and a very small key. That was all.

'Well, I don't know what use these are going to be,' said Micky dolefully. 'A feather, a button and a key!'

'Sh!' said Pam suddenly. 'Can you hear something?' Micky stood still and listened. He heard a whispering coming through the keyhole of the locked door. It must be Tumpy.

'Stroke the canary with the red feather!' said the whispering voice. 'Stroke the canary with the red feather!'

Micky at once took the feather and stuck it between the bars of the golden cage. He began to stroke the canary with the red feather. He did it until he was quite tired, and then he asked Pam to take a turn too. So she stroked the canary for a long time. But he didn't make a movement and he didn't sing a note. It was disappointing.

'That horrid big goblin will be back again soon,'

sighed Micky, still stroking the canary. 'Oh, I wonder if this is any use.'

Just as he said that the canary gave a tiny chirruping noise. Then it suddenly took the red feather in its beak and tucked it into the silvery feathers that grew from its throat. Micky watched in surprise.

The canary hopped up and down in its cage. Then it opened its mouth and began to sing. How it sang! It was the loudest song the children had ever heard! The door burst open and in came Bom, looking very surprised and pleased.

'Well, well, I didn't think you'd do that so quickly!' he cried. 'The wizard Broody must have taught you a great deal of magic! Now come and change my sack of stones into gold for me! Ho, ho! You shall have a great feast and two big precious stones for yourselves when your tasks are finished!'

The children left the singing canary and once more followed Bom, this time into a curious little room hung round with black curtains, embroidered with goldfish. In the middle of the room was a big sack. Bom pulled it open at the neck. It was full of stones.

'Here you are,' he said. 'Change these into gold for me. I'll go away again if you don't like me to watch you.'

He went out and banged the door. Once more Micky ran to it and tried it – but no, it was fast locked. He stared in despair at the sack. Then he looked behind all the curtains to see if there was a door or window, but there wasn't. The only light came from a great lantern hung from the low ceiling.

'Micky! There's that whispering again!' said Pam in a low voice. Micky rushed to the door and listened.

Once more a tiny whisper came through the keyhole. 'Put the shiny button in the sack. Put the shiny button in the sack.'

'It must be Tumpy again,' said Micky gladly. 'What a good thing we were able to help him make that magic lemonade, Pam!'

He took the golden button from his pocket and

slipped it in the sack. It fell down between the stones and disappeared. Micky watched to see what would happen, quite expecting the stones to turn at once to gold. But they didn't.

The children watched and watched them – but they still remained grey stones. They were afraid Bom would come back – and goodness me, just as they were thinking he surely must be back soon, they heard the door opening. It was Bom!

Micky shut the sack quickly, hoping that he and Pam could slip out of the door before Bom could see the stones had not changed to gold. But the wily Bom had locked the door behind him!

He pulled open the sack – and to the children's great amazement they saw that the stones had changed to shining gold after all! There they were, yellow and bright. They must just have changed as the goblin came into the room.

'Smart children!' said Bom, pleased. 'Clever children! I didn't think you'd be able to do that! I shall write and tell your father you are very clever indeed. Now come and light the candle that won't light! Then you shall have a grand feast, and go home with two fine emeralds in your pockets!'

Micky and Pam followed him to yet another room, this time set with many sunny windows. On a pink table was a tall golden candlestick and in it stood a pink candle.

'This is a witch's candle,' said Bom. 'If only I could light it, it would burn for ever. Light it for me. I will leave you alone for a while.'

Out he went and locked the door behind him. Micky ran to listen to any whispering that might come – but oh dear me, Bom must have come back and caught poor Tumpy at the keyhole, for hardly had the whispering begun than there came the sound of an angry voice. Then somebody began to cry and was hustled away.

'That was poor old Tumpy, I expect,' said Micky. 'Now we shan't know how to light that witch-candle!

Well, I've only got one thing left, and that's a little key. I'll see if I can do anything with that.'

He took it out and ran it up and down the candle. Then he struck a match from a box lying nearby and tried to light the candle. But no, it wouldn't light. Micky did everything he could think of, but it wasn't a bit of good. Nothing would make that strange pink candle come alight. Pam was looking out of one of the windows. Not one of them would open, but she was looking out to see what lay beyond. There was a wonderful garden set with big, brilliant flowers, and flying about were the brightest, strangest birds she had ever seen. Pam stared as if she couldn't believe her eyes. Then she saw something else.

'Micky!' she called. 'Come here! Look at these two children coming up the path to the house.'

Micky looked. The children both had on pointed hats, and long, sweeping cloaks on which were embroidered moons, suns and stars. They carried long golden sticks in their hands.

'Goodness!' cried Micky suddenly. 'They must be the wizard's children – the ones he mistook *us* for! *Now* what are we going to do! Bom will soon know we are not the right children, and he will be very angry! Oh dear, whatever shall we do!'

Pam looked wildly round the room – and suddenly her eyes caught sight of a very small door, not more than eighteen inches high, set at the foot of one of the walls.

'Look, Micky!' she cried. 'There's a tiny door over there! Do you think we might perhaps open it and squeeze through?'

Micky looked – and in a moment he was down on his knees trying to open it. But it was locked! He groaned.

'Try that tiny key you've got!' whispered Pam in excitement. 'It might fit!'

Micky tried it, with trembling hands. It fitted! He turned it in the lock and pushed open the door. And at that very moment there came an angry voice outside the room, and the children heard the big door opening.

'I'll punish them!' cried Bom's voice. 'Telling me they were wizard children when they weren't! I'll make them my servants for a hundred years! Ho, ho!'

Micky pushed Pam through the tiny door and then squeezed hurriedly through it himself, just as Bom rushed into the room. The angry goblin saw them going through the little door and he rushed over to them. But he was far too big to get through it himself!

'I'll go round the other way and catch you!' he roared.

The children found themselves in a low passage. They stumbled along – and suddenly Micky felt a little hand in his and a voice spoke to him.

'Don't be afraid, it's only me, Tumpy! I've come to guide you to the looking glass room. If we're quick we shall get there before Bom does.'

Micky was so glad to have Tumpy! He hurried along with him, Pam following close behind. Down long twisty passages they went, in and out of funny little rooms, upstairs and downstairs and once through a dim, dark cellar. It was terribly exciting.

At last Tumpy pushed them into a room that seemed very familiar. Yes, it was the looking glass room at last! It was just like their nursery. Over on the wall was the long mirror.

'Quick! Quick! He's coming!' cried Tumpy, and the two children heard the sound of hurried footsteps and a loud, angry voice. Micky rushed to the mirror and leapt through it. He helped Pam through, and then suddenly thought of dragging the little goblin Tumpy through too. It seemed such a shame to leave him behind to the cross and unkind Bom. So he pulled the goblin through as well!

Micky looked round. He was in his own, proper nursery. How glad he was! So was Pam. Micky looked into the glass. He saw Bom the big goblin suddenly appear there, shaking his fist at them. Then he faded away, and Micky could see nothing but the reflection of his own nursery. Not even the funny little goblin chair was there now.

Tumpy heard footsteps outside the nursery door and he jumped out of the window. 'I'll come back again tonight!' he whispered.

Nurse came into the room, smiling. 'Well, have you been good children?' she asked.

'Oh yes,' said Micky. 'We've had a lovely time!'

'That's splendid,' said Nurse. 'Well, it's stopped raining, so you can go out. Go and get your rubber boots.'

They went, and when they were in the dark hall cupboard, putting on their boots, Micky spoke to Pam in a low voice. 'Did it really happen, Pam? Or did we imagine it? *Did* we go through that looking glass?'

'Yes, rather!' said Pam. 'Anyway, Tumpy came back with us. You can ask *him* if it was true or not when he comes to see us tonight! What an adventure we've had!'

And now they are waiting to see Tumpy again. I *wish* I could see him too!

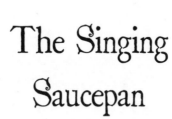

The Singing Saucepan

The Singing Saucepan

ONCE UPON a time there lived a pixie called Skip who made his living by selling tiny saucepans. He used to go about Fairyland, his saucepans hanging down his back in a string, their long handles sticking out all over the place.

They were good little saucepans and he made quite a lot of money out of them. But he was an impudent, cheeky little pixie, and many people couldn't be bothered with him. Then Skip would pull an ugly face at them and go on his way, singing a cheeky song.

One day he had sold no saucepans at all, and he was feeling very hungry.

'I really must get a penny or two somehow,' he said to himself. 'I am so *very* hungry! Ha! Here's a cottage! Perhaps the old dame who lives here will buy one.'

He went up to the front door and knocked boldly.

'Who is it?' cried a voice.

'Skip, the saucepan pixie!' said Skip. 'Will you buy a fine new saucepan?'

'No,' said the voice, 'I don't want one. Please go away because I'm busy.'

The cheeky little pixie pushed open the door and peeped in. He saw an old dame bending over her oven, looking at a fine cake she had just made. The sight made Skip's mouth water.

'*Do* buy one of my saucepans!' he cried.

'Didn't I tell you to go away?' said the old woman in a temper. 'Be off with you now! I'm busy!'

'Well, cut me a slice of that cake!' said Skip.

'Certainly not!' cried the old dame. 'Why, the king is coming to tea with me today, and I've made the cake for *him*!'

'Pooh!' said Skip. 'I don't believe *that* fine tale! What, the king will come to tea with an ugly old dame like you? Never!'

That made the old woman so angry that she rushed at Skip and gave him the soundest scolding he had ever had. He ran howling out of her cottage, his saucepans clanking behind him.

'The horrid old woman!' he sobbed, as he sat down behind a nearby hedge. 'I'll just punish her for that, I will!'

He sat and thought how he might revenge himself on the old dame, and at last he smiled a cunning smile. He took one of his saucepans and put it on the ground. Then he searched about till he found a curious little plant with a white flower and a black root. This he rubbed inside the saucepan, round and round and round, muttering magic words all the time.

He stayed beneath the hedge until the afternoon, and then he peeped into the kitchen of the old dame's cottage. It was empty, for she was in her bedroom, having a nap. The pixie stole in, whipped up the saucepan standing on the stove, emptied the water from it into his own saucepan, and then popped it on the stove, taking the old dame's saucepan away. Then he stole off again, hiding himself underneath the windowsill outside to watch the fun.

When the water in my saucepan begins to boil, what a shock the old lady will get! thought the mischievous pixie in delight. But just then his heart nearly stopped beating, for who should come driving up to the gate but the king of Fairyland himself, in a fine golden carriage!

'So the old dame told me the truth after all!' said the pixie, turning very pale. 'Ooh! How I wish I hadn't put the saucepan there with that naughty spell inside!'

He looked round to see if he could escape, but the king's coachman was standing by the gate and Skip did not dare to show himself. He peeped in again through the window.

The king was now sitting down at the old dame's

table, talking kindly to her and eating a slice of her new-made cake.

'This is a very nice cake,' he was saying – when suddenly a loud voice began singing in the saucepan on the stove! The water was boiling and the spell was beginning to work.

> *'The old woman here*
> *Is a miser I fear!'*

sang the voice.

> *'She's ugly and mean,*
> *The worst ever seen,*
> *She's not even clean,*
> *Her eyes they are green,*
> *She hasn't a friend . . .'*

The saucepan went on and on singing rude and untrue things about the surprised old dame, who couldn't *think* where the voice was coming from. As for the king he stared round in astonishment, a very angry look in his eyes.

'It's the saucepan!' he cried suddenly and ran to the stove. He lifted it off the fire, and as soon as the water went off the boil the singing voice stopped its naughty song.

'Someone's been playing a bad trick on you,' he said. 'Is this your saucepan?'

The old woman looked closely at it.

'No!' she said in surprise. 'Oh, I know! It must belong to that saucepan pixie who wanted me to buy a saucepan from him this morning, and was very rude to me when I said I didn't want one. He must have stolen into my kitchen when I wasn't here and popped that singing saucepan in the place of mine. Oh, the wicked little thing!'

'He shall be punished!' cried the king in a rage, and he jumped to his feet again. At these fierce words the pixie outside the window shivered and shook.

Then he took to his heels and ran, almost knocking down the coachman standing by the gate.

Down the lane he tore, his saucepans clanking behind him. The coachman ran after him, but the pixie soon left him out of sight and ran on and on for many a mile.

I shan't be safe till I'm out of Fairyland, he thought as he ran. *Oh, good! There are the gates!*

He rushed out of the big golden gates and ran on into our land till he came to a big oak tree. He sank down to rest under the spreading branches. His saucepans clanked loudly.

I'd better get rid of my lovely saucepans, thought Skip sorrowfully. *If I don't, people will easily know me, and I might get caught and taken back to be punished.*

So he stood up and shook them off his back. He looked round for somewhere to hide them. He thought that the best place would be up in the leafy greenness of the oak tree. So he threw them all up into the tree and then went on his way.

Where he went to, nobody knows – but the oak tree was delighted with the tiny saucepans.

'Just the thing to sit my acorns in!' it said to itself. 'Now why didn't I think of something like that before?'

So it sat each of its acorns in one of Skip's saucepans, and there they were, as safe as could be. And from that very day the oaks have always put their acorns into little saucepans, whose handles are stuck firmly on to the twigs until the time comes for them to drop to the ground.

Have you seen them? You really must look at Skip's nice little saucepans next time you see acorns on an oak tree!

Dame Crabby's
Surprise Packet

Dame Crabby's Surprise Packet

DAME CRABBY lived on the outside of Tipkin Village, and the little folk who lived there were very glad that she didn't live right in the village itself. She was a cross old dame, and as lazy as could be. Her cottage was dark and dirty, and spiders simply loved to weave their cobwebs in every corner.

Tipkin Village was a very spick and span place. The steps to each cottage were as white as snow, the little gardens were full of bright flowers and the curtains at each window were always clean.

Tipkin Village was trying to win the prize that the king of Fairyland gave each year for the best kept village. Jinkie the gnome and Popple the pixie went round every day to remind all the little folk to weed their gardens, keep their chimneys swept, wash their curtains, whiten their front steps and shine up their door knockers.

But, of course, nobody could do anything with old Dame Crabby. She just simply would not do what she was told. She kept her steps disgracefully – they were really black with dirt. As for her windows, you couldn't even see through them to know if her curtains were clean or not. Her garden was a mass of weeds, her chimney smoked, there wasn't a clean spot in the whole of her cottage and Dame Crabby herself looked like a bundle of old clothes.

'She'll prevent us from winning the prize,' groaned Jinkie and Popple. 'It's a shame. Dame Crabby, it is mean of you. Won't you at least try to be clean and tidy?'

The funny thing was that Dame Crabby didn't seem to see that her cottage was dirty!

'What's the matter with it?' she would ask. 'Didn't I sweep up the floor this very morning? And didn't I pull up a thistle yesterday?'

'Oh dear, that's not nearly enough to keep a house and garden tidy and neat!' sighed Jinkie. 'Look here, Dame Crabby, will you go out for the day, to visit your cousin Sarah? Then we'll all come in and make your cottage and your garden simply beautiful.'

'Well, I don't mind doing that,' said Dame Crabby. So it was arranged that she should go the next day and catch the half-past eight bus.

But of course she overslept and missed the bus and then she wouldn't go. The little folk were almost in tears about it.

'I can't think what you are worrying about,' said Dame Crabby crossly. 'Anyone would think my cottage was dirty to hear you talk. I really can't see anything the matter with it and I never shall. Do go away and leave me in peace.'

The little folk went away sadly. They had brought

brooms and dusters, scrubbing brushes and mops, meaning to have a good clean-up if only Dame Crabby had gone to visit her cousin. But it was no use now.

'I'll go and ask Mr Tubby, the wise man in the next village, if he can help us,' said Jinkie at last. 'He may have a good idea.'

So off he went. He told Mr Tubby his trouble, and the little, round wise man listened. He sat and thought for a long time, and then he got up from his chair and took a little blue box from a cupboard.

'I'll send her a spot of sunshine,' he said. 'Sometimes a spot of sunshine will show people how dusty and dirty things are, when nothing else will. I'll pack it into this pretty box in the form of a golden star that shines brightly. Dame Crabby will wear it as a brooch. It will be a great surprise for her!'

He drew a circle round a ray of sunshine that lay on the table. He muttered a few magic words, and when the sun went behind a cloud and the sunshine fled, a little spot still lay on the table, winking and blinking away brightly in the circle of chalk. It was like a little golden star, very beautiful to see.

Carefully Mr Tubby picked it up and slipped it inside the blue box. He tied it round with string and gave it to Jinkie, who was very grateful.

'Post it on your way home,' said the wise man. Jinkie thanked him and said goodbye. He stopped at the post office and posted it to Dame Crabby. Then he went home to Tipkin Village to tell all the little folk there what he had done.

The next morning the blue box arrived at Dame Crabby's. How surprised she was, for she never got parcels or letters! She opened the box and had an even greater surprise – for the sunshine star shone out so brightly that it dazzled her eyes!

'Goodness me!' she cried. 'What a lovely thing! It's a brooch, the finest ever I saw! Now who in the world has sent me that?'

She put it on the front of her dress where it shone like a little lamp. How pleased the old dame was! She took up her knitting and sang a little song to herself, she was so happy. Then she dropped her ball of wool, and down on the floor she went to look for it.

The spot of sunshine shone into the dark corners there, and my, how dirty they were! Dame Crabby was shocked.

'Bless us!' she cried. 'I'd no idea the floor was so dirty! I must scrub it!'

So she scrubbed it till it shone as white as snow. Then she went to the larder to get herself a bit of bread and cheese – and the sunshine star shone brightly into that dark cupboard, showing up grey cobwebs in the corners, stale spots of grease on the dirty shelves and crumbs all over the place.

Dame Crabby stared in surprise.

'Well, who would have thought my larder was so dirty!' she cried. 'Just look at that! I must certainly clean it today!'

So she set to work and cleaned it out. It took quite a time, for it was really dreadfully dirty. It looked beautiful when she had finished. The sunshine star shone round it and the shelves gleamed white and the cobwebs were all gone. Dame Crabby was pleased.

When she went to bed that night she put the spot of sunshine on the chest beside her. It shone on to the bedclothes and she saw that they wanted washing. It shone on to her dress over the bed rail and she saw that it wanted mending. It shone on to her washstand and dear me, how cracked and old the basin and jug looked!

'I must do some shopping,' said Dame Crabby, before she fell asleep. 'I want some nice new things. Ho, ho! Those folk down in Tipkin Village wanted to come and clean out my cottage, did they, and make it as spotless as theirs? Well, I'll show them a thing or two! I'm richer than any of them, and I'll go and buy the prettiest curtains in the kingdom and a fine new dress of red silk for myself, and a new basin and a jug of blue china, and – and – and . . .'

But by that time she was fast asleep.

Dame Crabby put on her sunshine brooch the next day, and once again it lit up the dirty corners. In the morning she cleaned and scrubbed and in the afternoon she went shopping. My, the things she bought!

She was so pleased with herself in her dress of red silk that she thought she would give a party. But first she went poking and prying into all the dark corners of her cottage, the sunshine star lighting up every cobweb, every bit of dirt and every speck of dust. It was marvellous, really! Dame Crabby was so pleased with herself for finding the dirty corners; she didn't for one moment think it was the sunshine brooch she wore!

All the little folk of the village were watching and waiting to see what would happen – and how delighted they were to see that the spot of sunshine was doing its work!

'If only Dame Crabby would see what a mess her garden is in, everything would be all right!' they said.

Well, that very morning Dame Crabby took a chair

into the garden to have a rest, for she felt a little tired. And her sunshine brooch shone into the tangled weeds and lit up a lovely red rose, almost choked by nettles and thistles!

Dame Crabby saw the rose glowing there.

'Dear, dear!' she said. 'Look at that wonderful rose trying to bloom in that mess of weeds. I must pull them up so that it can bloom properly. It's a very lovely rose.'

Then the spot of sunshine fell on a patch of sweet williams, trying in vain to poke their bright heads above the weeds. Dame Crabby saw them too, and up she jumped. She began to weed! My, what a lot she pulled up! Then she thought she would cut her grass and weed the path too.

By the time she was ready to give her party, her cottage and her garden were just as fine as anyone else's. She sent out her invitations, asked Matty Mouse to come and help her hand round the cakes and pour out the tea, and put on her fine new dress of red silk.

All the folk of Tipkin Village came to her party – and how they praised her new curtains, her new carpet and her lovely new eiderdown! Nobody said anything at all about the spot of sunshine gleaming on Dame Crabby's dress, but they all chuckled to themselves to think how that little speck of sunlight had made such a change in the old dame's cottage!

Just as they were sitting down to tea, there came the sound of galloping horses – and who should arrive in Tipkin Village that sunny afternoon but the king of Fairyland himself, come to see if the village was well kept enough to win the prize. He was so surprised when he found everyone out – but he had a good look at all the empty houses and was delighted to see them so pretty and neat.

Then he drove to the only house in the village that had smoke coming from its chimney, and that was Dame Crabby's – and in at the front door he walked and sat down with all the astonished and delighted folk to have a cup of tea and a slice of Matty Mouse's brown gingerbread. Goodness, what an excitement there was!

Well, of course, Tipkin Village got the prize, and it was a big sack of gold.

'We must take ten pieces of it to Mr Tubby, the wise man!' cried Jinkie and Popple.

'But why?' asked Dame Crabby in surprise. 'He hasn't had anything to do with our winning the prize!'

'Oh yes, he has!' cried Jinkie, pointing to the sunshine brooch gleaming on the old dame's dress. 'We got that from him – and it made you clean up your cottage and make your garden as nice as anyone else's!'

Well, at first Dame Crabby frowned to think of the trick that had been played on her – but when she looked round and saw her pretty new curtains, her nice silk dress and all the laughing folk of Tipkin Village eating her lovely tea, she was glad and she laughed too. She took off the sunshine star and gave it to Jinkie.

'I shan't need it any more,' she said. 'Give it to someone else!'

So Jinkie keeps it to send to people who are not as clean and tidy as they should be. I don't want it to be sent to me, but I'd love to see it, wouldn't you?

The Very Beautiful
Button

The Very Beautiful Button

CINDERS THE gnome had three beautiful buttons. One was green, one was blue and one was yellow. He always had them sewn on the front of his tunic, and was very proud of them indeed.

He was a bad-tempered fellow, and not many of the folk in Crab-Apple Village liked him. He was rich and knew a good deal of magic, so most people were frightened of him.

One day there was a concert in the village hall and Cinders made up his mind to go. It looked rather like rain, so he took his big umbrella with him, but he didn't need to put it up because the rain didn't come after all, and he reached the hall quite dry.

He took his place in the middle of the seats and listened to the concert. Halfway through he heard a loud pop and he looked down to see what had happened.

The middle button had come off his tunic! Cinders must have had rather too much dinner and the button had burst off. It was the yellow one that Cinders liked best of all.

He looked down at the floor, but he couldn't see it. He didn't like to disturb everyone by getting up to look for it, so he just sat still, waiting for the end of the concert, when he could look for it.

When the concert finished, there was tea for everyone in the hall, and soon there was a lot of chattering and laughing. Cinders began to look for his beautiful yellow button. But although he hunted under all the chairs and searched all round about his seat, he could *not* find his precious button.

'Someone's picked it up and stolen it,' said Cinders

fiercely. So he clapped his hands loudly and made everyone stop talking and look round.

'I've lost one of my very beautiful buttons,' said Cinders, frowning hard. 'I can't find it, so someone must have taken it. Please come and give it to me at once.'

Nobody moved. Cinders frowned still more.

'Ho!' he said. 'So you won't give me back my button! Well, I'll soon be able to find the thief, so he needn't think he will get away with my button! Now come! Let me have it back before I use my magic spells to find out who has it.'

Still nobody moved or said a word, although everyone looked as frightened as could be. Then Cinders got very angry indeed and took a piece of green chalk from his pocket.

He drew a big circle on the ground and put a dot in the middle of it. Then he put the chalk back into his pocket and took a little black wand out instead. He waved this in the air seven times, to and fro, and chanted a long string of powerful magic words, making everyone shiver with fright.

Then he clapped his hands three times and said loudly, 'Whoever has the button must now step into the middle of this circle!'

All the pixies and brownies looked at one another fearfully, wondering who would have to step into the magic circle. Cinders looked too – but to his great surprise, no one came forward at all. This was strange! Why didn't his spell work?

Once more he chanted his magic words, wondering if he had done something wrong, or missed a word out – but still no one came to step into the circle, and at last Cinders had to give it up. He was very angry, and very much puzzled too, for he couldn't think *why* his spell didn't work.

He put on his hat, took up his umbrella which he had hung on a chair back, and made his way to the door. Everyone looked at him, wondering what had happened to the beautiful button and why the spell hadn't worked. When Cinders got to the door he frowned crossly.

It was pouring with rain! What a nuisance! With everyone still watching him, he put up his big umbrella – and bump! Out of it fell his beautiful yellow button, hitting him on the nose and then dropping to the ground with a little tinkling noise.

'Ooh! It was in his umbrella all the time!' cried a hundred little voices. 'Ha, ha, ho, ho! It was in his own umbrella, and he didn't know it! It popped off and fell inside it and the foolish old thing didn't think of peering there! Oh, silly Cinders – oh, what a joke! It hit him on the nose!'

Well, that's just what *had* happened! When the button had popped off, it had slipped inside Cinders' umbrella, which he was holding in front of him – and he had never once thought of looking there! And of course, when he opened it, out fell the button!

How ashamed of himself Cinders was! He hung his head, blushed very red, and then ran home as fast as ever he could.

And now nobody is frightened of him at all, and when they meet him they say, 'Good morning, Cinders, and how is your beautiful yellow button today?'

But I think he deserves to be teased, don't you?

The Escape Spell

The Escape Spell

ONCE UPON a time, when Spick and Span were playing in the meadow, old Witch Snoogle came along and tried to catch them. Spick disappeared down a rabbit hole – but the witch caught Span and carried the little brownie off to her castle. She locked him up in a room until she was ready to make him help her with her spells.

Span was most unhappy. He sat and moped – and then he almost jumped out of his skin! Someone had thrown a big book through the bars of the open window! It fell with a crash on to the floor. Span picked it up. It was a book of magic! He ran to the window and looked out and, peeping out of a rabbit hole, he saw Spick!

'Find an escape spell!' called Spick, and Span nodded his head. He turned over the pages until he came to the Escape Spell. It was a very strange one. Span read it through two or three times and then shook his head! He would never be able to do this spell! He read it out loud:

'Take a cup of butter, the tooth of a lion, the beard of a goat and the golden eye of day. Mix them together and say the most magic word you know. Then you will see a way of escape.'

'Now, how can I get a lion's tooth?' sighed Span. 'And what goat would give me its beard? I might get the cup of butter – but who knows where the golden eye of day is to be found?'

After a while the Snoogle witch called Span to help her with her spells. The brownie sulkily followed her. As he was doing her bidding he saw that she had a vase of wild flowers on her table, and he looked at them – and as he looked he grew red with excitement. He began to see how he might do the escape spell! When the witch was not looking he took four of the flowers out of the vase. Who knows what they were? Aha!

He hurried to his room with the four flowers. One was a daisy. One was a buttercup. One was a goat's beard – and the last was a dandelion!

'I guess I can do the spell with these!' said Span in excitement. 'A cup of butter – well, here is a buttercup! Won't that do? The tooth of a lion – well, here's a dandelion – and, as everyone knows, its name means *dent-de-lion*, which is French for tooth of a lion! Its leaves are toothed, and so it has that peculiar name! The beard of a goat – well, here is the pretty goat's beard flower; surely that will do! And what about the golden eye of day? Won't a daisy do? Its name means day's eye and it has a pretty golden heart. Now what is the most magic word I know?'

Span thought hard. Then he nodded his head. He

had thought of a very magic word indeed. He took the buttercup, the dandelion, the goat's beard and the daisy and mixed them together. He called out his magic word.

Crash! The bars across his window fell out and clanged to the ground. His way of escape was clear! Span leapt out of the window and ran to the rabbit hole. Spick was there waiting and pulled him to safety.

'Good old Span!' cried Spick, as they hurried home. 'I knew you'd find the way to escape!'

Could you have done the same, do you think? Well, you'll know what to do if you're ever a prisoner. But don't forget to say the magic word, will you!

Too-Tiny,
the Gnome

Too-Tiny, the Gnome

ONCE UPON a time there was a little gnome called Too-Tiny. He was a surly fellow, bad-tempered and mean. Nobody liked him, and he had been driven away from three different villages. So now he lived all alone, grumbling and muttering to himself, planning what he would do if only he could get rich.

And then one day he found a great treasure cave! Goodness, what sacks of gold there were! Too-Tiny could hardly believe his eyes. He looked into this sack and that one – yes, they were all full of gold.

'It must have been a robber's treasure cave,' said Too-Tiny to himself in glee. 'Ha, now I'm rich! Now I can do everything I want!'

The very first thing he did was to take one of the sacks of gold on his back and go to Witch Green-Eyes. He left the sack behind a bush in her front garden and then knocked at her door.

'What do you want?' asked the witch, opening her door.

'I want to know how much you will charge me for a giant spell,' said Too-Tiny.

'What do you mean?' asked Green-Eyes in astonishment.

'Well, I want to make myself the size of a giant,' said Too-Tiny. 'I am tired of being small. No one takes any notice of me. So I want a giant spell.'

'Oh, I see,' said the witch. 'Well, giant spells are terribly expensive, Too-Tiny – far too expensive for *you*!'

'You tell me how much one costs, and I will pay you,' said Too-Tiny crossly.

'Well, I should want a whole sack of gold,' said

the witch, shutting the door with a bang.

'Open the door, open it, I say!' shouted Too-Tiny, thundering on it with his fists. 'I've got the money here! Give me the spell, Green-Eyes.'

The witch opened the door again and looked at the little gnome in amazement.

'*You've* got a sack of gold?' she said. 'Why, where is it? I shan't believe you unless you show it to me.'

Too-Tiny ran to the bush and dragged out his sack. He opened it, and the surprised witch saw all the gold inside. She went indoors and came out with a bottle in her hand, full of green liquid.

'Leave me the sack of gold,' she said, her green eyes shining at the thought of so much money. 'Here is the giant spell. Mix it with sour milk and drink it on the next full moon night. Then you will shoot up to the size of a giant!'

Too-Tiny snatched at the bottle, put it carefully into his pocket and ran off with it. When he got home, he looked at it.

'Ho!' he said in glee. 'When I'm a giant, I'll go and live in a big castle on the top of Breezy Hill above the village of Tick-Tock and won't I give the people a fright! I'll make them do this and that for me, and I'll see that they all obey my slightest word! What a time I'll have! Instead of being Too-Tiny the Gnome, I'll be Too-Big the Giant!'

On the next full moon night, Too-Tiny mixed the spell with sour milk and put it into a mug. Then he went out into the moonlight and drank it.

Ooh! What a funny feeling came over him! He felt growing pains all up his arms and down his legs, his head felt as if it were bursting, and his fingers and toes tingled with pins and needles!

And all in a moment he shot up to the size of a giant! Goodness, what a strange sight that was to see! An owl nearby got such a fright that it fell off the tree it was perching in, and flew away *too-whooing* at the top of its voice.

Too-Tiny felt a little bit frightened at first when

he found that everything looked much smaller to him. But he soon got used to it, and strode over the fields and back again in delight, using his long legs to take great strides over ponds and rivers.

'Ha!' he said, when he was tired of trying his long legs. 'I'm a giant all right now! But it's time I went to sleep. Tomorrow I'll make my plans.'

He couldn't sleep in his cottage, for he was far too big. So he lay down outside the treasure cave and was soon snoring loudly there.

The next day he set about having a castle built for himself. In a short time he had a hundred little workmen toiling night and day on Breezy Hill, and in three weeks they had built a monstrous castle. The people of Tick-Tock village were a little afraid when they saw such a huge giant walking about, but they felt sure that he would take no notice of them.

Soon Too-Big, as he was now called, had settled into his new castle, and had carefully carried all the gold of the treasure cave into the strong cellars underneath the castle itself. Then he began to make himself a nuisance to the people of Tick-Tock village.

He frightened the children, and scared the grown-up folk by walking heavily down the narrow street, making their houses shake from top to bottom. He quarrelled with Mr Biscuit the baker, and trod on his house, so that it broke to pieces – and then he wouldn't pay the poor man a penny-piece to get it mended.

When six of the villagers went to his castle to demand that he should pay some money to Mr Biscuit, Too-Big lost his temper and shouted so loudly at them that they all went home crying. Oh, he was a dreadful person to have in a peaceful village!

Too-Big ate such a lot that he needed plenty of cooks to see to his food, and plenty of servants to look after him. He paid good wages, and as the little village of Tick-Tock was poor, many of the villagers had to go to the castle to work for Too-Big.

He was very unkind to them, and treated them

badly. If they didn't do exactly what he wanted, he pulled at their noses and ears. They couldn't fight him because he was so big, so they just had to put up with it.

But how they grumbled!

'If only we could get rid of him!' they said to one another. 'If only he would go! We won't work for him any more! We'd rather be poor than get good wages at the castle.'

So one day Too-Big found himself alone in his big castle, with not a single servant to cook his dinner or see to his wants. He was very angry, and he went down to the village and picked up twenty little folk at once.

'Ho! So you think you'll get the better of me, do you?' he shouted. 'Well, you won't! I'll just carry you back to your work, and if you run away again, I'll throw you up to the moon!'

Too-Big liked to keep a list of all the money he spent, but he was very bad at adding up and made such a lot of mistakes that his sum book was nothing but crossings out and holes where his rubber had gone through the page. He wouldn't have anyone to help him, for he didn't wish any of the villagers to know how rich he was.

'How can I get all these sums right?' he wondered, as he sat one day at his big table, trying to add up all he had spent in the last week. 'Every time I add up the figures they come to a different answer.'

Then suddenly a good idea came into his head.

'Why, of course!' he said. 'I'll go to old Witch Green-Eyes again and buy a magic pencil from her, one that will add up all my sums by itself without a mistake! Now why didn't I think of that before!'

Off he went to Witch Green-Eyes, a sack of gold over his shoulders. He rapped on the roof of her house, for he was too big this time to bend down to her little door, and the witch looked out of the window in surprise.

'Oh, it's Too-Tiny,' she said. 'Well, what do you want this time?'

'I'm *not* Too-Tiny,' said the giant crossly. 'I'm Too-Big. I've come for a magic pencil that will add up my sums by itself without a mistake. I'm always getting them wrong.'

'You can have one for that sack of gold,' said Green-Eyes, and she handed a curious yellow pencil to Too-Big. It had a red tassel at the end, and this tassel was never still, but shook and wagged as if it were alive.

'Here's the gold,' said Too-Big, and put it down in the garden. He put the pencil into his pocket and strode off, feeling pleased with himself.

It *was* a wonderful pencil too! As soon as Too-Big sat down and put it on his sum book, the tassel wagged itself like mad, and the pencil added up all the figures and put down the answers with never a single mistake. Too-Big thought it was marvellous, and the pencil was his greatest treasure. He was always setting it sums to do, and it was never tired of doing them. All his bills were added up correctly, and Too-Big was delighted.

And then one day, when he put his hand in his pocket for the pencil, it wasn't there! He searched in this pocket and in that, but he couldn't find it. He hunted all over the room, but still he couldn't see the wonderful pencil.

Then he set all his servants hunting for it, but *they* couldn't find it either.

'It *must* be found!' said Too-Big in a fearful rage. 'If it isn't, I'll throw you all up to the moon, every one of you! So hunt now, hunt! If one of you has stolen it, I'll *certainly* throw them up to the moon!'

Well, all day long the little folk hunted, but it wasn't a bit of good. That yellow pencil was nowhere to be found. Then Too-Big called everyone into the big hall and looked at them solemnly.

'I am sure one of you has stolen my wonderful pencil,' he said. 'I don't know who the thief is, but I shall soon find out. I have been to Witch Green-Eyes and bought a fly-away spell from her. Here it is, in this little box!'

He showed it to all the astonished people.

'Now!' he said. 'This is what I am going to do. I am going to empty the powder in this box over a candle and say two magic words – and whoever has my pencil will at once be spirited away by magic to the great enchanter who lives among the Mountains of the Moon. And you know what *that* means, don't you? He will make you his servant and never will he let you go.' All the little people groaned and wondered who had the pencil – but nobody said a word.

Too-Big lit a candle, and then carefully emptied the powder in the box over the flame, saying two magic words out loud.

The candle flame shot up to the roof, and dense smoke came from it so that everyone began to blink their eyes and choke and cough. The smoke spread all over the room so that no one could see anything. When it cleared away the little folk looked at one another to see who had been spirited away.

But no one had! Every servant was there, for they had counted. They looked at one another in surprise.

'Well, none of us had the pencil!' they cried. 'Who does then?'

'Where's Too-Big gone?' asked the tallest pixie there. 'He's vanished!'

So he had! There wasn't a sign of him to be seen. The little folk couldn't make it out.

Then suddenly Tippitty, the very smallest pixie, began to laugh loudly.

'Ho, ho, he, he!' he chuckled. 'I'll tell you something! Too-Big had the pencil himself! He had been using it, and when he had finished, he stuck it behind his ear and forgot all about it! I saw it there just before he put the powder on the candle, but I wasn't going to tell him! Let him go to the moon, I thought!'

Then all the little people began to talk and laugh at once! What fun! Too-Big had spirited himself away! He hadn't guessed that his pencil was behind his ear all the time, and he had worked the fly-away spell on himself.

'By now he'll be with the enchanter in the Mountains of the Moon!' everyone chuckled. 'Oh, what a joke!' He'll never come back here again, and we shall be happy once more!'

Sure enough, when Too-Big had spoken the magic words and had emptied the powder over the candle flame, he had disappeared. A great wind had taken hold of him, and he had shot out of the window. The next thing he knew was that he was sitting down – bump! – in front of a strange higgledy-piggledy castle set among the Mountains of the Moon.

The bump sent the yellow pencil away from where he had stuck it behind his left ear, and it clattered to the ground beside him – and in a trice Too-Big knew what he had done! He was full of dismay!

'Oh! Oh!' he groaned. 'Of course, I put it behind my ear and then forgot – and now the fly-away spell has acted on *me*, and I'm on the moon!'

Soon the great enchanter himself came out to see who had come to his castle, and when he saw it was a giant, he was delighted.

'Why, you're just the person I want to build me a bridge over the nearest river,' he said. 'There's a lot of heavy carrying to do, and you will be able to do it easily.'

So Too-Big was set to work – but although he had the great body of a giant, he had still only the strength of a gnome, and he couldn't carry even one heavy stone without groaning under its weight.

The enchanter thought he was lazy and shouted at him, but soon he saw that the great giant really had no strength at all.

'You're no use to me!' he snorted angrily. 'Whoever heard of a giant who couldn't carry stone for a bridge? I've a good mind to turn you into a dog. You'd be more use to me then!'

'Please don't!' begged Too-Big. 'I'm not really a giant, but only a little gnome. I found a cave full of treasure and bought a giant spell from Witch Green-Eyes. That's how I became a giant – but I'm not really, so don't make me work so hard, or I shall surely die.'

When the enchanter heard this, he found it difficult to believe at first. But he knew how to find out if Too-Big was telling the truth.

He took a peacock's feather and dipped it into black treacle and white milk. Then he hit Too-Big smartly on the head with it, saying, 'If a giant, then stay a giant. If a gnome, then be a gnome!'

At once Too-Big shrank almost to nothing and to his horror was no bigger than he had been before, when he was Too-Tiny. The enchanter looked at him and laughed.

'Yes, you spoke the truth,' he said. 'You are not a giant, but a mean-looking little gnome. Well, you're not much use to me, so if you would like to give me all your treasure, I'll give you your freedom, and you shall go back to Earth again.'

At first Too-Tiny wouldn't hear of such a thing, for he couldn't bear to think of all his treasure going to the enchanter of the moon. But his master made him work so hard and treated him so badly – just as badly as Too-Tiny had treated *his* servants at the castle – that soon he went to the enchanter and begged him to let him go.

'You shall have all my treasure,' he said. 'But let me go free, I'm begging you.'

The enchanter called a shooting star and the two climbed into a carriage which was hitched by a silver rope to the star. Then in a trice they shot to Earth and landed just beside the castle in which Too-Tiny had lived when he was a giant.

He showed the enchanter all his treasure and the magician rubbed his hands in glee.

'Get out of this castle,' he said to Too-Tiny. 'I'm going to take it and the treasure back to the moon with me.'

Too-Tiny ran quickly out of the castle and watched

to see what would happen. Suddenly there came a rumbling noise, and the whole castle rose in the air and flew rapidly upwards, getting smaller and smaller as it disappeared from sight. Too-Tiny watched till he could see it no longer, and then he sighed heavily.

'There goes all my treasure!' he said. 'And my castle! And I'm no longer a giant, but a gnome again, with not a single friend. How unhappy I am! There is nothing left for me to do but to work for my living!'

He went down to the village of Tick-Tock, and there the kindly little folk, who did not guess that the gnome was no other than the giant they had once hated so much, did their best to help Too-Tiny.

Too-Tiny was grateful. He worked hard and even learnt how to smile. He saved a little money and bought a tiny cottage at the end of the village.

'Now I'm going to turn over a new leaf!' he said. 'I won't be cross and surly, I'll be kind and good, and I'll see if that makes me any happier.'

Well, of *course* it did, and would you believe it,

plump little Dame Round-Eyes fell in love with him and married him. Now they're as happy as can be and have five dear little children. And when they ask Too-Tiny for a story, he tells them about the time when he was Too-Big the Giant.

But of course they don't believe him!

The Magic Sweetshop

The Magic Sweetshop

JO AND Tom were going over Breezy Hill for a walk when they saw a narrow path going off to the west that they had never seen before.

'Hello!' said Tom in surprise. 'I've never seen that path before. Let's see where it leads, shall we, Jo?' So off they went down the funny narrow path. Little did they know that it was to be the beginning of a very strange adventure!

After a while they came to what looked like a tiny village – just three or four cottages set closely on the hillside with two shops in the middle. One of them was a funny little shop with a small window of thick glass. Behind the panes were tall, thin bottles of brightly coloured sweets.

'A sweetshop,' said Jo, surprised. 'I didn't know there was one on this hill, did you, Tom?'

'No,' said Tom. Jo pressed her nose to the window and looked at the bottles of sweets. She cried out in surprise as she read their labels.

'Tom! These are very strange sweets! Just read what they are!' Tom looked at the labels, and certainly the names of the sweets were very strange indeed. The blue sweets were labelled GIANT-SWEETS, and the pink ones TINY-SWEETS. There were lots of other kinds too.

'You know, this must be a magic shop,' said Jo excitedly. 'Let's go in and buy some! I've got a sixpence piece and so have you.'

So they pushed open the door and went inside. At first they thought there was nobody there, but then they saw a small knobbly-looking man sitting behind the counter. He had a strange tuft of hair growing straight up from his head and two long, pointed ears. His nose was long and pointed too. He was sitting by himself reading a bright blue newspaper. 'What would you like this morning?' he asked, folding up his newspaper neatly.

'Could we have sixpence worth of mixed sweets each?' asked Tom eagerly.

'Certainly,' replied the shopman, twitching his pointed ears like a dog. He took four bottles from the window and emptied some sweets on to his scales. Jo looked at the labels on the bottles so that she would know which sweets were which. She saw him place a giant-sweet, a tiny-sweet, an invisible-sweet and a home-again-sweet into the scales.

The children felt very excited when the shopman handed each of them a bag. He took their money and put it into a tin box. Then he picked up his blue newspaper and began to read again.

'What will happen to us if we eat these sweets?' Tom asked the little man, but all he would say was,

'Try, and see!'

The children didn't like to ask him anything else so they went outside and walked up the little crooked street. They were surprised when they came to a big white gate that went right across the road.

'This is stranger and stranger,' said Tom. 'I've never seen that village before, and now here is a gate that I've never seen before either.'

'Shall we climb over?' said Jo. 'We are nearly at the top of the hill.'

'Yes, let's,' said Tom. To their great surprise, they saw a town on the other side!

'How strange!' said Jo. 'There has never been anything on the other side of this hill before!'

They went on down towards the town, and soon met some most peculiar-looking people. They were very round and their arms were very long indeed. Their faces were as red as tomatoes and they wore big white ruffs round their necks, which made their faces seem redder than ever.

Some of them were riding in small motorcars, rather like toy ones but with sunshades instead of proper hoods. Jo and Tom stood in the middle of the road and stared in astonishment.

A motorcar with a bright yellow hood came along at a tremendous pace. Tom jumped to one side, but Jo was just too late and the little car ran right into her. To her great amazement it exploded into a hundred pieces!

The little round man in the car shot up in the air and down again. He landed on the ground with a bump and he *was* cross!

'You silly, foolish, ridiculous girl!' he cried. 'Why didn't you get out of my way? Look what you've done to my car? It's gone pop!'

'Well,' said Jo, getting up. 'I'm sorry, but you were driving too fast. You didn't even hoot.'

'You horrid, nasty, rude, selfish girl!' cried the little man, getting even crosser.

'Hey!' said Tom. 'Don't speak to Jo like that!

Haven't you any manners? You might have hurt her very much running into her like that!'

The little round man went quite purple with rage. He took a trumpet from his pocket and blew loudly on it. *Tan-tara! Tan-tara!*

At once a whole crowd of funny-looking people came running up and took hold of Jo and Tom.

'Take them to prison!' shouted the man whose motorcar had exploded. 'Give them nothing but bread and water for sixty days!'

The children could do nothing against so many, so they were marched off to a big yellow building and locked up in a tiny cell. Tom banged on the door but it was no use. It was locked and bolted on the outside.

'Look here, Jo!' said Tom suddenly. 'Let's eat one of these sweets each. Perhaps something will happen to help us!'

So they each picked a blue sweet from their bags and put it into their mouths. And before long a very curious thing happened! They began to grow taller.

Yes, and wider too! In fact their heads soon touched the ceiling.

'I say! Those must have been the sweets out of the giant-sweet bottle!' said Tom in excitement.

He kicked at the door and it almost broke, for his feet were now very big.

'Stop that!' cried an angry voice outside. 'If you kick your door again, prisoners, I shall not give you any supper!'

'Ho!' said Tom, pleased. 'I shall certainly kick it again! Then when it's opened, Jo, we'll walk out and give everyone a shock!'

Bang, bang, bang! He kicked the door hard again. At once it was unbolted and unlocked and a very angry keeper came in. But when he saw how big the children were, his red face turned quite pale and he ran away as fast as his little legs would carry him!

Tom and Jo squeezed out of the door and went down the street. How they laughed to see the astonishment on the faces of the townsfolk, who now looked very small indeed.

Soon they came to a crossroads. There was a signpost and on it was printed: TO GIANTLAND.

'Goodness!' said Jo. 'How exciting! We are giants now, Tom. Do let's take this road and see if we can find some other giants.'

So the children set off, feeling more and more excited. After half an hour they came to some enormous trees and realised that they must have arrived in Giantland.

Soon after that they saw a giant – but dear me, the giants were far bigger than the children had guessed they would be! In fact, they were enormous! They towered over the children.

A very large giant with eyes like dinner plates saw them first. He gaped at Tom and Jo in surprise and then called to his friends nearby in a voice like thunder, 'HEY! LOOK HERE! HERE ARE SOME STRANGE CHILDREN!'

Immediately the children were surrounded by a

dozen huge giants. They didn't like it at all. One of the giants poked his finger into Tom's chest.

'HE'S REAL,' he said in a booming voice. 'HE'S NOT A DOLL.'

'Of course I'm not a doll!' shouted Tom crossly. 'Don't poke me like that!'

It amused the giants to see how cross Tom was, and they poked him again and again with their big bony fingers.

'Aren't they nasty, unkind creatures,' cried Jo, for she didn't like the great giants with their enormous eyes and teeth like piano keys. 'Oh, Tom, can't we escape?'

'How can we?' said Tom, trying to push away a finger that came to tickle him. 'Oh, I know, Jo! Let's eat another sweet!'

In a great hurry the children took out their sweet bags and ate a pink sweet each. In an instant they felt themselves growing smaller and smaller, smaller and smaller. The giants seemed to grow bigger and bigger and bigger. Soon they were so big that they seemed like mountains! The children were tinier than sparrows to the giants – tinier than ladybirds even!

'Quick!' said Jo, catching hold of Tom's hand. 'Let's go somewhere safe before they tread on us!'

There was a large hole in the ground not far from them and Jo and Tom ran to it. It seemed like a dark tunnel to them, but really it was only a wormhole!

Down the tunnel they went, meeting huge worms and other giant creatures as they went. A great beetle hurried by them, treading heavily on Jo's toes. It was all rather alarming.

'I wish we could get out of here,' said Tom, after a time. 'Oh look, Jo! There's a tiny pinhole of light far ahead of us. That must be where the wormhole ends. Come on!'

On they went and at last came out into the sunshine on a green hillside, and nearby was a notice saying:

BROOMSTICK HILL
ALL TRESPASSERS WILL BE
TURNED INTO SNAILS

'Ooh!' said Jo in alarm. 'Look at that!'

But they hardly had time to read the notice before there was a strange whirring noise up above them. To the children's enormous surprise about a hundred witches came flying through the sky on broomsticks. They darkened the sky like a black cloud.

The witches were heading for the green hillside and, of course, the very first thing their sharp eyes saw was Jo, with her golden-yellow hair. Tom had hidden quickly behind a bush, but Jo was so surprised to see the witches that she hadn't even thought of hiding!

As the witches came rushing over towards them, Tom pulled Jo down beside him.

'Get out your sweet bag and eat a sweet!' he

whispered. 'We've got two left. Eat the purple one and we'll see what happens!'

'Where is that trespassing child?' cried the witches. 'We will turn her into a snail! How dare she come to our hillside!'

Jo and Tom popped the purple sweets into their mouths. They looked around – and to their surprise they couldn't see each other. At first they didn't know what had happened, and then they guessed – the sweets had made them invisible!

The children ran off down the hill. When they looked back at the witches, they were hunting in astonishment all around the bush where they had seen Jo.

'There's no one here!' they cried. 'Where has she gone?'

By this time Jo and Tom were at the bottom of the hill. As they could not see one another, they held each other's hands very firmly.

'I'm tired of this adventure,' said Jo, at last. 'We

always seem to be chased by something – funny people, or giants or witches. Goodness knows what it will be next time! Can't we go home now, Tom?'

'But we don't know the way,' said Tom, looking around. 'I'm hungry and I'd love to go home. I wish I did know the way! However are we going to get home again, Jo?'

'I know,' said Jo, feeling for her sweet bag. 'Let's eat the last sweet, shall we, Tom, and see what happens.'

So the children put their last sweet – a red one – into their mouths and before they had finished eating it they could see one another again! They were so pleased, for they were both tired of being invisible!

Tom and Jo waited patiently to see what else would happen. Would a big wind come and carry them home? Or perhaps a fairy carriage pulled by butterflies would arrive to help them. They waited and waited, but nothing happened. They looked at each other and sighed.

Jo and Tom just went on sitting there at the bottom

of the hill, waiting in the sunshine. But still nothing happened. It was very strange.

Perhaps the home-again-sweets wouldn't take them home after all? If not, how would they get there? They were quite sure they would never be able to find the way by themselves!

Then Jo began to look around her. She saw a big fir tree that she seemed to know. She noticed a house not far off that looked familiar, and she was sure she recognised the pathway leading up the hill. Suddenly she jumped up with a cry of delight.

'Tom! We are home! This is the hill just outside our own garden! That's our house over there! Why, we've been home all the time and didn't know it! However could we have got here? I'm sure the hill outside our garden isn't really a witch's hill.'

They were astonished, but it was quite true – they really were home again. They were just outside their own garden. They could see their mother standing at the front door.

'Well, how surprising!' said Tom, standing up and brushing himself down. 'We're safely back after our adventures. Let's go and tell Mum. Perhaps she'll come with us this evening and see that funny sweetshop on the hillside.'

The children ran home and told their mother all about their strange adventures. That evening they all went up the hillside to find the sweetshop. They followed the little path – but alas, it did not lead to a sweetshop at all; only to a great many rabbit holes!

'It's just a rabbit path!' said Mother. 'You must have dreamed it all, my dears!'

But they didn't really, you know!

The Tale of Higgle and Hum

The Tale of Higgle and Hum

ONCE UPON a time the king of Fairyland went to his magic cupboard and found that a thief had been there in the night.

'My goodness!' cried the king loudly. 'Robbers! Now what have they taken?'

He called the queen and together they went through all the things in the magic cupboard, and they found that three things had been stolen.

'There's my magic lamp gone!' said the king in dismay. 'The one that lights up the whole of the wood when the moon doesn't shine for our dances.'

'And where are my magic scissors?' said the queen

with a groan. 'The pair that will cut through anything – iron, steel or stone!'

'And my fine walking stick,' said the king sadly. 'I'm sorry that has been stolen, because I had only to say, "Up, stick, and at him!" and it would jump up and defend me.'

'How shall we get our things back?' wondered the queen. 'And who has taken them?'

They soon found out who the thief was. It was a goblin called Groo, a cunning fellow who had long wanted these three things for himself.

'He is so clever that I am afraid we shall never have our magic things again,' said the queen with a sigh. 'If we sent our soldiers against him, he would simply turn them all into an army of ants, and that would be dreadful.'

'Well, we'll send out a proclamation saying that if anyone can get back our magic things for us we will give them a sack of gold, a beautiful palace and a free invitation to all our dances and parties,' said the king.

So this was done, and soon all the elves, pixies, fairies, gnomes and brownies were talking excitedly of how the three things belonging to the king and queen might be taken from Groo the goblin.

First an elf tried, and, oh dear me, he was turned into a frog, and it took the king a very long time to find the right spell that would change him back into his own shape again. Then two gnomes tried and they were turned into earwigs. They went to the king in a fright, and he had to pay a wise man twenty pieces of gold to change them back again.

After that no one tried, for everyone was afraid. Then one day there came wandering into Fairyland two imps called Higgle and Hum. As soon as they heard of the king's message they looked at one another in delight.

'*We'll* get the things back!' they cried.

'Easier said than done!' said a listening brownie. 'You don't know how clever Groo the goblin is!'

Higgle and Hum said no more, but went off to a

sunny hedgeside to talk about how they should get into Groo's house.

'We've been poor and ragged all our lives,' said Higgle, 'and we've never had a chance of being rich, or having nice shoes and clothes. Why, we haven't even been to a party or a dance! How fine it would be to have a sack of gold and live in a palace on a hill! And oh, think of going to every single party that the king and queen give! What a fine time we should have!'

'How shall we get the magic things, though?' asked Hum. 'Hadn't we better make a plan?'

They thought and thought, and at last decided that it wasn't a bit of good making a plan – they had just better see what they could do and make plans as they went along.

That night they crept into the garden of Groo's house and peered in through the kitchen window.

'Look!' whispered Higgle. 'There's the magic lamp on the dresser!'

'And there are the magic scissors in that workbasket!' said Hum. 'Where's the magic stick?'

'Standing in the corner yonder,' whispered Higgle. 'Oh! Oh! Oh!'

It was no wonder he cried out for someone had suddenly caught hold of him! It was Groo the goblin, and very soon he had Higgle in one hand and Hum in the other, both imps trembling with fright.

'Ho!' he said in a harsh voice. 'What are you doing peeping and prying into my kitchen, I should like to know? Don't you know that I can turn people into earwigs and frogs, if I want to?'

'Please, please don't do that!' said Higgle in a fright. 'We were thinking what a nice warm kitchen you had and wondering if you wanted any servants.'

'Well, my wife could do with two,' said Groo. 'I'll show you to her and see if she wants you. If she doesn't I'll have you cooked for my dinner.'

He took the shivering imps into his kitchen and showed them to his wife, who looked at them through her big glasses.

'Yes, they'll do nicely, dear,' she said to Groo. 'I'll have them for servants.'

'Well, if you get tired of them, let me know and I'll have them cooked for dinner,' said Groo. 'And mind, wife, don't you let them get away! They'll run if they have a chance, I'm sure of that. You keep them safely in the kitchen.'

'Very well, dear,' said Mrs Groo, and she turned to Higgle and Hum. 'Just draw some hot water from the tap and start to scrub the kitchen floor,' she said.

Groo the goblin went out of the room and banged the door. Higgle and Hum ran to the tap and got a pail of water. It was not very hot, and Higgle looked at the fire.

'Please, ma'am,' he said to Mrs Groo, 'the water isn't hot enough to scrub the floor properly. The fire has gone down and the water is cooling. Shall I stoke it up?'

'Oh dear, oh dear, there's no wood in the woodbox,'

said the old dame in a flurry. 'I meant to have asked Groo this morning to chop some for me, and I quite forgot. What a temper he will be in when I ask him now, for he does hate to go out to the woodshed in the dark.'

'Well, ma'am, let *me* go,' said Higgle. 'I'm your servant, aren't I?'

'Of course!' said Mrs Groo. 'Well, out you go and chop me some wood – but don't be long.'

Higgle grinned at Hum and ran out. He didn't go to the woodshed, but hid outside the front gate. Soon Mrs Groo became impatient and wondered what Higgle was doing.

'Drat the imp!' she said. 'I suppose I must go and see if he's lost his way in the garden.'

'Ma'am, let *me* go and find him!' said Hum, running over to her. 'Don't you go out in the darkness! Lend me that lamp on the dresser and I'll soon find him!'

'Well, take it, and don't be long,' said Mrs Groo. She lit the lamp and Hum took it. He ran out into the garden, puffed out the lamp, and made for the front gate. He found Higgle there, and together the two clever imps raced down the lane as fast as their legs would carry them, rejoicing that their trick had succeeded.

The king was delighted to get his magic lamp back, and he praised the two imps for being able to outwit the cunning old goblin.

'If only you can get the other things I shall be overjoyed!' said the queen.

So the next night Higgle and Hum made their way quietly to Groo's house again, meaning to break in at the window when Groo had gone to bed, and take the scissors and magic stick. But the goblin was lying in wait for them, and pounced on the two scared imps just as they reached the front gate.

'Ha!' he said. 'Now I've got you again, and I can tell you, I won't let you go *this* time! I'll have you for my dinner tomorrow!'

He dragged the imps into the kitchen and shut

them into the woodbox for the night. They could not get out, and they trembled there in fear, thinking that their end was very near this time. In the morning Mrs Groo took them out and looked at them.

'You are very naughty not to have come back the night I sent you to chop the wood,' she said. 'Now I've got to cook you for my husband's dinner, instead of having you for servants!'

The imps watched her stoke up the fire and trembled all the more. Then Higgle spoke.

'I suppose, ma'am, you've got plenty of killy-kolly leaves to cook with us?' he said. 'If imps are cooked without killy-kolly leaves, they will poison whoever eats them.'

'My goodness!' said Mrs Groo in fright. 'No, I didn't know that! Well, I've plenty of killy-kollies in my garden. I'd better go and pick some.'

'Let *me* pick them for you,' said Higgle. 'You've plenty to do in preparing the dinner, I'm sure.'

'All right, you may go and pick them,' said Mrs

Groo, giving him a plate. 'But see that you keep in sight of the window, for if you run off again, Mr Groo will be very angry.'

Higgle took the plate, grinned at Hum and ran out into the garden to the killy-kolly bed. He began to pick some of the leaves, and he pretended that they were very hard indeed to pull from the stems. Mrs Groo became impatient and called out of the window to him.

'Hurry up, now, hurry up! I'm waiting for that dish of leaves. What a time you take picking them!'

'Please, ma'am, they're very hard to pick,' said Higgle, standing up in the killy-kolly bed. 'Could you send Hum out with a pair of strong scissors? Then I could cut the leaves off easily and bring them in to you at once.'

Mrs Groo went to her workbasket and took out the pair of magic scissors there. She gave them to Hum and bade him take them to Higgle and then come back to help her peel some potatoes. Hum ran off, and as soon as Higgle saw him coming he ran to the front gate, and down the lane the two imps tore as fast as they could.

How glad they were to be free and to have the magic scissors! They took them to the king and he was delighted.

'You're a very clever pair!' he said. 'Now if only you can get me my magic stick, I shall be very happy.'

The two imps didn't dare to go near Groo's house now, for they knew he would be on the watch for them. But at last, after ten days had gone by, Higgle and Hum went once more to the goblin's house, and this time they crept in at the back door.

But oh dear me, who should spy them but old Mrs Groo, and she caught them and dragged them into her kitchen.

'So it's you again!' she said. 'Well, you ran away last time with the magic scissors, and the time before with the magic lamp – but this time you *won't* get away! Mr Groo was angry with me for letting you go, but he will be pleased with me now for catching you!'

'Where *is* Groo?' asked Higgle, looking round.

'He's gone to see his friend, Mr Topple,' said Mrs Groo, 'but don't you fret! He won't be long, I can tell you, and I shouldn't be surprised if he has you for his supper as soon as he comes home.'

Higgle and Hum were frightened. They felt quite sure that they really would be eaten this time, and they tried in vain to think of some way of escape.

Mrs Groo sat down to her sewing, and for some time there was silence in the warm kitchen. Then the clock struck nine, and Mrs Groo looked up in surprise.

'Dear, dear!' she said. 'How late Groo is! I do hope he hasn't got lost on this dark night.'

'Shall I go and look for him?' asked Higgle.

'No, that you won't!' said Mrs Groo sharply.

'Well, ma'am, just let me go to the front door and peep out,' said Higgle. 'You can see I don't escape then, can't you, but as I have very sharp eyes,

I can see a long way and could tell you if your husband is coming.'

'Very well,' said Mrs Groo, 'but mind – if you so much as put a foot over the doorstep, I'll drag you in and put you into that saucepan, Higgle.'

Higgle grinned at Hum and went to the door to open it. He stood on the doorstep and peered this way and that. Suddenly he gave a shout.

'Robbers! Thieves!' he cried. 'Look! Robbers, thieves! Where's a stick! Bring a stick to defend me!'

Mrs Groo began to tremble. She picked up the magic stick that stood in the corner and gave it to Hum, who ran to Higgle with it.

Sure enough, someone was coming up the front path, and Mrs Groo felt certain it must be robbers. She began to scream.

'Up, stick, and at him!' shouted Higgle, and at once the stick leapt from his hand and flew at the person coming up the path. How he yelled and shouted.

'I'm no robber, I'm Groo the goblin! Call the stick

off, call it off! I'm Groo the goblin, I tell you!'

But Higgle and Hum shouted too, so loudly that Mrs Groo couldn't hear that it was her husband in the garden and not a robber. She hid herself in a corner and didn't dream of calling the stick off.

Higgle and Hum ran to the back gate and halfway down the lane, grinning to think that the wicked goblin was tricked again.

Then Higgle put his hands to his mouth and shouted loudly,

'Stick, stick, come to me!'

The stick flew to Higgle's hand. The two imps set off running as fast as they could and the goblin could not catch them, but could only stumble into his kitchen and sit down on a chair.

How delighted the king and queen were to see their magic stick safely back again!

'Surely you are the two cleverest imps in the kingdom!' said the king. 'Well, you shall have your sack of gold and your palace, and you may be sure you will receive a free invitation to every party and dance that the queen gives. Thank you very much for all you have done.'

Then in delight the two imps took the gold and went to the palace that the king gave them. They bought themselves splendid new suits, took two wives and lived happily in their glittering palace for ever after. They still go to every party in Fairyland, and though they must have been to thousands now, they haven't got tired of them yet!

As for Groo the goblin, he was so ashamed at being tricked by two imps that he packed up his things and he and Mrs Groo disappeared, nobody knew where – and nobody minded either!

Slip-Around's
Wishing Wand

Slip-Around's Wishing Wand

ONCE UPON a time there was a great magician called Wise-One. He was a good magician as well as a great one, and was always trying to find spells that would make people happy and good.

But this was very difficult. He had made a spell to make people happy – but not good as well. And he had found a spell that would make them good – but not happy too. It wasn't any use being one without the other.

Now one day he found a marvellous way of mixing these two spells together – but he hadn't got just one thing he needed.

'If only I had a daisy that had opened by moonlight, I believe I could just do it!' said Wise-One, as he stirred round a great silvery mixture in his magic bowl. 'But whoever heard of a moonlight daisy? I never did!'

Now just at that moment, who should peep into his window but Slip-Around the brownie. When he heard what Wise-One was saying, his eyes shone.

'Wise-One, I can get a daisy that has opened in the moonlight,' he said.

'What!' cried Wise-One in delight. 'You can! Well, there's a full moon tonight – pick it for me and bring it here.'

'What will you give me if I do?' asked Slip-Around.

'Oh, anything you like!' said Wise-One.

'Well, will you give me your wishing wand?' asked Slip-Around at once.

'How do you know anything about my wishing wand?' said Wise-One.

'Oh, I slip around and hear things, you know,' said the brownie, grinning.

'You hear too much,' grumbled Wise-One. 'Well, as I said you could have anything, you can have that – but only if you bring me the daisy!'

Slip-Around ran off. He meant to play a trick on the magician! He didn't know where any daisies were that opened in the moonlight – but he knew how to make a daisy stay open!

He picked a fine wide-open daisy, with petals that were pink-tipped underneath. He got his glue pot and set it on the fire. When the glue was ready he took the daisy in his right hand and a paintbrush in his left.

Then, very daintily and carefully, Slip-Around glued the petals together so that they could not shut. He put the daisy into water when it was finished and looked at it proudly. Ah! That would trick Wise-One all right! He would get the wishing wand from him – and then what a fine time he would have with it!

When night came the daisy tried to shut its petals – but it could not, no matter how it tried, for the glue held them stiffly out together. So, instead of curling them gently over its round yellow head, the daisy had to stay wide open.

Slip-Around looked at it and grinned. He waited until the moon was up, and then went to Wise-One's cottage with the wide-open daisy. The magician cried out in surprise and took the daisy eagerly. He put it into the water.

'Good!' he said. 'I'll use that tomorrow – it's just what I want for my spell.'

'Can I have the wishing wand, please?' said Slip-Around shyly. He didn't mean to go away without that!

Wise-One unlocked a cupboard and took out a shining silvery wand with a golden sun on the end of it. He gave it to Slip-Around.

'Use it wisely,' he said, 'or you will be sorry!'

Slip-Around didn't even say thank you! He snatched the wand and ran off at once. He had got a wishing wand! Fancy that! A real wishing wand that would grant any wish he wanted!

He danced into his moonlit village, shouting and singing, 'Oh, I've got a wishing wand, a wishing wand, a wishing wand!'

People woke up. They came to their windows and looked out.

'Be quiet, please!' called Higgle, the chief man of the village. 'What do you mean by coming shouting like this in the middle of the night!'

'Pooh to you!' shouted Slip-Around rudely. 'Do you see my wishing wand? I got it from Wise-One!'

Nobody believed him. But all the same they leant out of their windows and listened. Higgle got very cross.

'Go home!' he shouted to Slip-Around. 'Be quiet – or I'll have you punished in the morning!'

'Oh no, you won't!' cried Slip-Around boastfully. 'I can wish you away to the moon if I want to! I know what I will do – I'll wish for an elephant to come and trample on the flowers in your silly front garden! Elephant! Come!'

Then, to everyone's immense astonishment, an elephant appeared round the corner of the street in the moonlight and began to walk over Higgle's lovely flowers. How angry he was!

Soon the folk of the village were all out in the street, in dressing gowns and coats. They watched the elephant.

'That is very wrong of you,' said Dame Toddle to Slip-Around.

'Don't interfere with me!' said the brownie grandly. 'How would you like a giraffe to ride on, Dame Toddle? Ha, ha! Good idea! Giraffe, come and give Dame Toddle a ride!'

At once a giraffe appeared and put the astonished old woman on its back. Then very solemnly it took her trotting up and down the street. She clung on to its neck in fright. Slip-Around laughed and laughed.

'This is fun!' he said, looking round at everybody. 'Ha, ha – you didn't think I really had a wishing wand, did you! Now where's Nibby – he scolded me the other day. Oh, there you are, Nibby! Would you like a bear to play with?'

'No, thank you,' said Nibby at once.

'Well, you can have one,' said Slip-Around. 'Bear, come and play with Nibby!'

Up came a big brown bear and tried to make poor Nibby play with it. Nibby didn't like it at all. When the bear pushed him in play, he fell right over.

'Now just stop this nonsense,' said Mr Spinny, stepping up to Slip-Around firmly. 'If you don't, I shall go to Wise-One tomorrow and tell him the bad things you have done with the wishing wand.'

'Ho, ho – by that time I shall have wished Wise-One away to the end of the world!' said Slip-Around. 'You won't find him in his cottage! No – he'll be gone. And I shall wish myself riches and power and the biggest castle in the land. And I've a good mind to make you come and scrub all the floors, Mr Spinny!'

'*Hrrrumph!*' said the elephant, and walked into the

next-door garden to tramp on the flowers there. It was Mr Spinny's! He gave a yell of rage.

'Mr Spinny, I don't like yells in my ears,' said Slip-Around. 'You yell like a donkey braying. I'll give you donkey's ears! There! How funny you look!'

Mr Spinny put his hands to his head. Yes – he now had donkey's ears growing there. He turned pale with fright. Everyone began to look afraid. It seemed to be quite true that Slip-Around had a real wishing wand. What a dangerous thing for a brownie like him to have!

The little folk tried to slip away unseen, back to their houses. But Slip-Around was enjoying himself too much to let them go.

'Stop!' he said. 'If you don't stay where you are, I'll give you all donkey's ears – yes, and donkey's tails too!'

Everyone stopped at once. Slip-Around caught sight of Mr Pineapple the greengrocer. 'Ha!' said the brownie. 'Wasn't it you that gave me a punishment the other day?'

'Yes,' said Mr Pineapple bravely. 'I caught you taking one of my apples and you deserved to be punished.'

'Well, I wish that every now and again a nice ripe tomato shall fall on your head and burst,' said Slip-Around. And immediately from the air a large ripe tomato fell on to the top of Mr Pineapple's head and burst with a loud, squishy sound. Mr Pineapple wiped the tomato juice out of his eyes. Almost at once another tomato fell on him. He looked up in horror, and moved away – but a third tomato fell from the sky and got him neatly on the top of his head.

Slip-Around began to laugh. He laughed and he laughed. He looked at the great elephant and laughed. He looked at poor Dame Toddle still riding on the giraffe, and laughed. He looked at Nibby trying to get away from the big playful brown bear, and laughed. He laughed at Spinny's donkey's ears. In fact, he laughed so much and so loudly that he didn't hear someone coming quickly down the street. He didn't see someone creep up behind him and snatch at the wishing wand!

'Oooh!' said Slip-Around, startled. 'Give me back my wand – or I'll wish you at the bottom of the village pond!'

Then he began to tremble – for who was standing there, frowning and angry, but Wise-One, the great magician himself!

'You wicked brownie!' said Wise-One sternly. 'You gave me a daisy whose petals were glued open so that it couldn't shut – not a real moonlight daisy. I have spoilt my wonderful spell. You have no right to the wishing wand. I shall take it back with me.'

'Oh, why didn't I wish you to the end of the world when I had the chance!' wailed Slip-Around. 'Why didn't I wish for riches, and power, and a castle – instead of playing about with elephants and giraffes and things!'

'Great magician!' cried Mr Spinny, kneeling

down before Wise-One. 'Don't go yet. Look what Slip-Around has wished for! Take these things away from us!'

Wise-One looked around in astonishment and saw the bear and the elephant and the giraffe and the donkey's ears on poor Spinny's head, and the ripe tomatoes that kept falling – squish – on to Mr Pineapple.

'I'll remove them from you,' he said to the listening people, 'but I'll give them to Slip-Around. He will perhaps enjoy them!'

He waved the wand and wished. The elephant at once went to Slip-Around's garden and trampled on his best lettuces. The giraffe let Dame Toddle get off and went into Slip-Around's house, where he chewed the lampshade that hung over the ceiling light. The bear romped over to the frightened brownie and knocked him down with a playful push.

The donkey's ears flew from Mr Spinny to Slip-Around – and lo and behold, the ripe tomatoes began to drop down on the surprised brownie, one after the other, until he was quite covered in tomato juice!

'You've got what you wished for other people,' said Wise-One with a laugh. 'Goodnight, everyone. Go back to bed.'

They all went home and got into bed, wondering at the night's strange happenings. They were soon asleep – all except Slip-Around. He had the elephant, the giraffe and the nuisance of a bear in his cottage with him – and it was terribly crowded! His donkey ears twitched, and he had to wipe tomato off his head every minute. How unhappy he was!

Poor Slip-Around! He had to sleep under an umbrella at last, and the giraffe ate up the tomatoes that fell down – plop! The elephant snored like a thunderstorm and the bear nibbled the brownie's toes for a joke. It was all most unpleasant. And somehow I think that Slip-Around won't try to cheat anyone again! What do you think?

Mr Pink-Whistle's Cat is Busy

Mr Pink-Whistle's Cat is Busy

ONE DAY, just as Mr Pink-Whistle was about to go and catch the train to visit his old aunt, Sooty, his cat, came running to him.

'Master – there's a black cat with white paws come to see you. He wants your help.'

'Well, Sooty, I can't miss my train,' said Pink-Whistle. 'See if *you* can help him. After all, you're a cat too, and you know my ways – you can surely put right whatever the cat has come about. You can use anything out of my spell cupboard if you like.'

'Thank you, master,' said Sooty, and waved goodbye to Pink-Whistle from the door. Then he shut it and went to the back door, where the black cat with white paws was waiting patiently.

'*I* will put things right for you,' said Sooty rather grandly. 'What's the trouble, Whiskers?'

'Well, it's the man next door,' said Whiskers. 'He's a thief, Sooty, and a very sly one. He only takes small things, usually what he can put into his pockets or carry in his hands. I've known about him for years, of course, but I've never bothered about him till today.'

'Why today?' asked Sooty, taking the cat indoors. 'Help yourself to the milk in my saucer – it's nice and fresh. Now tell me everything!'

'Well, I belong to a very kind old lady,' said Whiskers. 'But she's going a bit blind, and she can't see as well as she used to, and this man next door – Mr Gubbs his name is – keeps coming in, pretending to ask how she is, and each time he pops something into his pockets – perhaps a sausage roll from the larder, or a book from the bookshelf or even

240

something from my old lady's purse.'

'How wicked!' said Sooty. 'Just because the old lady can't see!'

'Yes. And this morning my old lady missed the stick she uses when she goes for a walk,' said Whiskers. 'It's a fine black one made of ebony, with a shining silver handle, and she's very proud of it. Now it's gone.'

'Did this Mr Gubbs take it?' asked Sooty.

'Of course he did! He came in to see the old lady this morning, and patted her hand and asked her how she was, and told her not to come and see him out of the door, he knew the way all right – and he took the stick out of the hallstand. He thought nobody saw him – but *I* saw him! I was sitting in a dark corner of the hall, watching.'

'It's a pity you aren't a dog,' said Sooty. 'Then you could bark at him and bite him.'

'I've tried hissing loudly, and putting out my claws if he comes near me,' said Whiskers. 'But he kicks me, and I'm afraid of him. Wouldn't Mr Pink-Whistle help? He likes to put wrong things right, doesn't he?'

'He's gone away. *I* can help instead,' said Sooty. He went to Mr Pink-Whistle's cupboard and looked at all the peculiar bottles and boxes there. He suddenly caught sight of a small bottle with blue-green liquid inside, and he laughed. He took it down.

'Look,' he said, 'this is a funny spell – it makes any tongue talk, and . . .'

'But that's silly – tongues always do talk,' said Whiskers.

'Not *all* tongues!' said Sooty. 'Not the tongues of shoes, for instance! Look, Whiskers, if you can manage to rub this spell on the tongues of Mr Gubbs' shoes, they will soon chatter away and tell the world about him – and *he* won't know who's doing the talking!'

Whiskers laughed so much that he fell into the saucer of milk. 'Give me the bottle,' he said. 'I'll manage to spread the spell on the tongues *some*how. Oh, what a time I'm going to have!'

He hardly waited to say goodbye to Sooty but ran off with the bottle in his mouth. And that night, when Mr Gubbs was in bed, and his shoes were in the kitchen, waiting to be cleaned, Whiskers hopped in at the scullery window and ran over to them. He poured a little of the blue-green liquid over the tongues of the shoes and then rubbed it in.

'Now, talk, shoes, talk as much as you like when Mr Gubbs wears you,' he mewed. 'Tell the world about him and what he does!'

Well, next morning Mr Gubbs put on his shoes as usual, and wondered where he could go that day to pick up a few more things that didn't belong to him. Yes – he would go round the market. It was market day, and there would be plenty of chances for him to take this or that.

So off he went. On the way he met Mr Jaunty and managed to take his nice blue silk handkerchief out of his pocket as he passed by. Then, when he passed Miss Jinky's house, he saw a lovely pink rose blossoming by the wall, and he snipped it off and put it in his buttonhole.

At the market he wandered round, smiling at people he knew, nodding politely, and stopping to say a few words to this person and that. He also managed to pocket half a pound of butter when Mrs Plump, who owned the butter stall, wasn't looking, and to put a handful of ripe white cherries into his pocket.

Then little Nicky and his sister came by and he offered them each a cherry from the ones in his pocket. 'Oh thank you!' said Nicky. 'Are they out of your garden?'

'Yes, I picked—' began Mr Gubbs, but another voice interrupted him. 'He took them from the cherry stall,' said the voice. 'Oh, he's clever, he is!'

'Pooh – call that clever?' said another voice. 'I call it cunning – sly and cunning!'

Mr Gubbs was extremely startled. He looked all round for the talkers, but there was no one near except the two children, and *they* were looking most astonished. They gave him back the cherries at once and ran off.

'Now look here – who said that?' began Mr Gubbs and heard a husky laugh somewhere near. It came from the tongue of his right shoe, but he didn't guess that, of course.

He went on his way, feeling puzzled and soon met Mr Burly, the farmer.

'Hallo, Gubbs!' said the farmer. 'Do you want to buy fresh farm butter. Go to my stall and—'

'He doesn't want any,' said a small voice loudly. 'He's got some in his pocket – it's a bit squashy.'

'He took it from Mrs Plump's stall when she wasn't looking,' said another voice. 'Oh, he's an artful one! He wants watching!'

'Er – good morning,' said Mr Gubbs to the astonished farmer and hurried off, his face flaming red. *Who* was it talking about him like this? He looked behind him. Was it some irritating children who had been following him? No – there was nobody near.

Old Lady Smiles came bustling up. 'Oh, good morning, Gubbs. My word, that's a beautiful rose you have in your buttonhole. What's its name?'

'Er – I think it's called Beauty,' said Mr Gubbs. 'I – er – picked it from my garden this—'

'He picked it off Miss Jinky's best rose bush when he passed by her garden this morning,' said a little voice quite clearly. 'Nobody was looking.'

'You can't believe a word he says!' said the second voice. 'Not a single word. Horrid old Gubby!'

The other shoe-tongue gave its husky little laugh. 'What about his blue silk hanky? *I* saw him take it out of Mr Jaunty's pocket. Did you?'

'Oh yes! I've just as good a view as you have of all his goings-on,' said the other shoe-tongue. 'I remember when . . .'

'Good morning to you, Gubbs,' said Lady Smiles stiffly. 'I don't know if you can hear what I can hear – but I must say that I think it's all very extraordinary. *Good* morning!'

It soon got around that there was something peculiar about Mr Gubbs that morning, and to his great disgust one person after another came up – just when he didn't want them! He must, he really *must* find out about those voices! As for the shoe-tongues, they had a perfectly marvellous time!

'Look, there's Mrs Grocer coming – she doesn't guess that old Gubby took a tin of biscuits from her shop last week! Hoo-hoo-hoo!'

'And here comes old Mr Whoosh. What would he say if he knew that Gubby took his tin of tobacco and popped it into his pocket, when he went calling on him the other day?' said the other tongue. 'It's no good his asking for it back either – it's all gone up in smoke!'

'Hoo-hoo-hoo!' laughed the other voice. 'You are very funny this morning. Ooooh, I say, look – here comes the policeman, and Gubby doesn't like the look of him!'

Indeed Gubby didn't! He was now so scared of what the extraordinary voices were saying that all he wanted to do was to run back home, shut his door and hide. But the policeman had been very, very interested in some of the things that the market folk had told him about Mr Gubbs, and he wanted to make a few inquiries.

Gubby began to walk away quickly, and the voices shouted loudly. 'He's scared! He knows he's got that butter in his pocket!'

'And his socks belong to Mrs Jinky's husband – he took them off the line the other night!'

'And he took the vest he's wearing too! And what about his watch? Wouldn't the policeman like to know about *that*! Hoo-hoo-hoo!'

Mr Gubbs took to his heels and ran, panting hard, hoping that the policeman hadn't heard a word. If only he could leave those voices behind! They must be somewhere in the market, nasty, mysterious voices. Once he got home he wouldn't hear them any more.

But he did, of course! As soon as he was indoors

and the door shut, he sat down, out-of-breath – and the first voice began again.

'He can run fast, can't he? My word, I got quite giddy, going up and down, didn't you?'

'Yes, I did. We shall have some more fun soon, though – the policeman will be along, and a few others. Old Gubby's going to get what he deserves at last, the mean old fellow. I never did like him, did you?'

'Why – it's my *shoes*!' shouted Gubby, and he took them off and ran out into the back yard. He took off the dustbin lid and threw in the shoes. Then back he went and put on his slippers. They had no tongues, thank goodness!

But it's no good, Gubby. There's a tramping down the street, and soon there will be a knocking at your door! You'll have to answer some very awkward questions, and when your house is searched you will find yourself marched off to the police station. So shiver in your slippers, Gubby – the time has nearly come. Ah – rat-a-tat-TAT!

Sooty, Mr Pink-Whistle's cat, was longing to know all that had happened, and he was very glad to see Whiskers coming along the next day, looking as if he were bursting with news.

'Sit down. Tell me everything!' said Sooty, and Whiskers began. He told the whole story – he related everything that the shoe-tongues had said, and he told how Gubby had at last been found out and taken to prison.

'How do you know all this?' asked Sooty, wiping tears of laughter from his eyes. 'Did you follow Gubby to market?'

'No. But, you see, he threw the shoes into the dustbin and I heard them talking to each other there, and went to rescue them. I took them out of the dustbin and they told me everything that had happened – every word they had said, and I laughed till my whiskers nearly fell off!'

'Where are they now?' said Sooty.

'Oh, they thought Mr Pink-Whistle might like to

lend them to someone else some day,' said Whiskers. 'So they walked here with me. They're outside the door. Thanks very much, Sooty, for helping to put a wrong thing right all by yourself. My mistress has got back her ebony stick and she is very happy.'

And off went Whiskers, grinning, very pleased with himself. 'Goodbye,' said a shoe-tongue as he passed the shoes. 'You certainly did us a good turn when you rubbed that blue-green polish into us – we've never had such a fine time in our lives. Thank goodness we don't belong to Mr Gubbs any more.'

'Nasty old Gubby! Hoo-hoo-hoo!' said the other tongue.

I can't imagine what Pink-Whistle is going to say when he comes back and finds those peculiar shoes. *Some*body will have a shock if Pink-Whistle offers to lend them to him! Just send a card to Sooty if you know anyone who ought to wear them!

The Goblin's Toyshop

The Goblin's Toyshop

'THERE'S A new toyshop at the end of the village!' cried the pixie children one day. 'Come and see!' So they all went, and pressed their turned-up noses against the toyshop window. 'Oooh,' they said in delight. 'What beautiful dolls! And look at that smart wooden soldier – and oh, that bear with twinkling eyes!'

'There aren't any trains,' said little Pop-Off mournfully. He did so like trains.

'And no bricks,' said Jinks, who liked building little houses.

'But see the sailor dolls and the baby dolls and the

dressed-up toy cats and dogs!' said Fenny. 'Oh, I wish my moneybox was full.'

The goblin who had just opened the new toyshop came to the door. He had bright green eyes and such pointed ears that they looked as sharp as arrows. He gave the children a grin that stretched from ear to ear.

'Well, children, I hope I shall see you on your birthdays and at Christmas time, and every Saturday too. You'll find my toys are far cheaper to buy than anyone else's!'

He was quite right. The pixie children could get a toy soldier for sixpence, and a big teddy bear with a growl in his middle for a shilling. The dolls were all the same price, a half crown each. It was marvellous.

It was no wonder that all the children of Cherry Village spent their money at the goblin toyshop. They bought dolls and soldiers and bears and dogs and cats. But they couldn't buy trains or bricks or ships or tops because the goblin didn't sell them.

'I'm not interested in those,' he said, with his wide grin. 'I only sell the toys I really like.'

And then, after he had sold a few dozen dolls and soldiers and bears, something peculiar happened. First Jinks's toy soldiers disappeared. Then Fenny's two new dolls went. Then Pop-Off's blue teddy bear vanished. Binkie's toy dog wasn't on the windowsill one morning, where he had left it the night before, and Gobbo's sailor doll had gone from the toy cupboard. How strange!

Nobody could find out what had happened. They hunted all over the place, but the toys were not found again. 'Some thief must have passed through our village in the night, and stolen all the children's new toys,' said the pixies mournfully.

The next night somebody's ragdoll disappeared, and three dolls. And then a toy dog vanished and a baby doll too. How very peculiar!

The pixies went to the goblin about it. 'Can you tell us what is happening?' they said, puzzled. 'Our children's toys are all going one by one.'

'Strange,' said the goblin, shaking his head. 'Very, very strange. I have no idea where the toys have gone – but as the children are so sad about it, please come to my shop with them and they shall have any toy they please at half price!'

'How kind you are!' said the pixies, pleased, and they bought a great many new toys from the green-eyed goblin. But before long those toys disappeared at night too, and nobody knew what was happening.

Then one night, little Fenny, who had three new dolls, decided that one of them had a bad cold and must be undressed and go to bed. So she took off all her clothes and her shoes and stockings, put a little nightie on her and popped her into bed.

That night two of her dolls disappeared – but not the one she had put to bed with a cold!

Her brother heard Fenny crying and came to see what the matter was. He looked puzzled when he heard that one of the dolls hadn't disappeared. Now why should the thief steal two, but leave the one in the cot?

'Fenny,' he whispered, 'I am going to watch for the thief! I shall hide in the wood and watch the lane that runs through the village. Whoever creeps down there at night will be the thief! I am sure he will have an armful of toys!'

'No – don't watch, Tippy,' said Fenny, frightened. 'You know everyone thinks it's a very powerful wizard, who comes at night and makes himself invisible so that no one sees him. And that's how he takes our toys – putting his invisible hand into our windows.'

'There's something strange about this,' said Tippy. 'I'm going to watch!'

So that night he hid in the wood and kept an eye on the lane that ran through the sleeping village. Nobody came. And then, just as Tippy was going to creep home, he heard a tiny sound. Tippitty-tap, tippitty-tap – and down the lane came a very tiny figure indeed. What could it be? A little wizard? A small magician?

Then he stared in astonishment. It was no wizard – but just a toy soldier, walking quickly down the lane in his little clicking shoes – tippitty-tap!

And then came a doll, and after that a soft-walking toy cat, dressed in a skirt and shawl. She had shoes on her feet, but she made no sound. Then came a curly-haired doll and two more toy soldiers! Tippy could hardly believe his eyes.

He called out in a whisper, 'Hi, soldier! Hi, sailor doll! What are you doing?'

But they took no notice at all. Not one of them even looked round, but went quietly on their way. They were toys that could walk, but they didn't seem to be alive.

Tippy got up quietly and followed a teddy bear down the lane. The bear walked steadily on, his shoes making a little shuffling noise because he didn't lift up his feet properly. And, to Tippy's great surprise, he walked in at the open gate of the goblin toyshop, went up the little path and in at the door. It must be open then!

Tippy crept up to the door too. It was ajar. Inside a tiny light was burning. One by one the toys went to a little shelf and sat themselves down. They were quite still then and didn't move at all.

Tippy looked round cautiously. He could hear someone snoring in the next room. That must be the goblin. He caught sight of a box with something printed on the lid. Tippy bent over it, trying to make out what was written there.

'Walking spells for shoes,' he read in astonishment, and then he suddenly guessed the secret of the disappearing toys!

That wicked goblin! He sold toys that wore shoes – he didn't sell trains or bricks or ships because they didn't wear shoes and couldn't walk. But soldiers and teddies and dolls could all wear shoes!

So he pops a walking spell into their shoes, knowing that

at a certain time the spell will work – and all the toys will walk back to him, so that he can sell them once again! thought Tippy. *Oh, he's bad. He's a fraud! But how clever he is!*

Tippy sat and wondered what to do. Then he caught sight of the goblin's boots standing by the door, and he suddenly grinned. He opened the box and took out a handful of the walking spells. He pressed them right into the toes of the boots. Then he crept out.

The next day everyone in the village knew about the goblin's mean trick. They crowded to his shop angrily, and he met them with his usual grin.

'What nonsense!' he said, when they had shouted to tell him what they knew. 'I know nothing about walking spells, nothing at all. I have never even heard of them. There are no such things. Tippy dreamt it all.'

'Pack up your things, you wicked goblin, and go!' shouted the pixies.

'Certainly not,' said the green-eyed fellow. 'I shall stay here as long as I like. Nothing can make me leave, and I warn you – be careful in case I put a bad spell on you all.'

But, as he spoke, his feet began to twist about and wriggle to and fro. The goblin gazed down at them in surprise. What was happening?

Tippy gave a chuckle. *He* knew. The handful of walking spells was beginning to work! And very soon the goblin found his feet walking him out of his cottage and down the path to his front gate. 'Stop, feet, stop!' he yelled. 'What's the matter with you?'

'The same thing that was the matter with the feet of all the toys you sold!' cried Tippy in delight. 'Walking spells in your boots – but I forgot, you've never heard of such things, have you?'

The pixies ran beside the furious, bewildered goblin till he came to the end of the village. Then they said, 'Goodbye! You've so many spells in your boots that you won't stop walking till you get to the Land of Goodness Knows Where! We shan't see *you* again, goblin!'

They didn't, of course, because he had to walk for years. What a wonderful time the children had in the toyshop!

'The toys are yours,' said Mr Plod, the policeman. 'The goblin cheated you of many dolls and other toys. Now take what you want. He will never, never come back.'

So the children took all the toys they wanted – but what was the first thing they did to them? Can you guess? Yes – they took off all the toys' shoes! They weren't going to have them walking away again!

Hooray for Shuffle the Shoemaker!

Hooray for Shuffle the Shoemaker!

'DO YOU know who's taken the cottage at the corner of the green?' said little Button, popping his head round Shuffle's kitchen door.

'No, who?' asked Shuffle, pricking up his pointed ears.

'Mr Pah!' said Button. 'And all I can say is I'm very glad I don't live in Tiptop Village! I couldn't bear to have Mr Pah poking his nose into my affairs, and saying "Pah!" to this and "Pah!" to that.'

Ma Shuffle looked dismayed. 'Of all the people we could do without in this village, Mr Pah is the one!' she said. 'I've met him before. He'll look in here and see what Shuffle's doing, and he'll say, "Pah! What an old-fashioned way to mend shoes!" And he'll look into my cupboard of spells and say, "Pah! Is that the best you have? What a poor lot!" He just takes the heart out of you, that magician.'

'Oooh, is he a magician?' said little Button.

'Yes, and a rich one too,' said Ma. 'He's often offered a sack of gold pieces to anyone who knows better than he does, but nobody's ever won it yet!'

'Oooh,' said Button again, and he looked at Shuffle. 'A sack of gold, Shuffle! I wish we had that!'

'Well, you'll never get it, Button, so forget it,' said Ma. 'Now here's the parcel for your mother. Get along with it, and keep out of Mr Pah's way if you can!'

Mr Pah was certainly a tiresome fellow. He looked in at Dame Scary when she was washing, and said, 'Pah! If that's the way you wash, I shan't ask you to do my things for me!'

He poked his nose in at Mr Clang the blacksmith's too. 'Pah!' he said. 'What silly little bellows you use to blow up your fire, no wonder it takes you ages to get it red hot.'

'Pah!' he said to Ma Shuffle. 'What a collection of old-fashioned spells you have! Haven't you ever heard of the new ones?'

'I'd like to know a spell that would stop people poking their noses in where they're not wanted,' said Ma in a dangerous kind of voice.

'Pah! That's easy,' said the magician. 'You just take a pinch of pepper, a sprinkle of—' And then he caught the glint in Ma's eye, and thought better of it. He backed out of the door. 'I might tell you another day,' he said.

'Yes, you do that,' said Ma. 'I could use a spell like that straight away!'

Well Mr Pah was so annoying that he really upset everyone in the village. 'Can't we get rid of him?' they said to one another.

'He's so clever,' said Dame Scary dolefully. 'There's no getting the better of him.'

Button and Shuffle put their heads together. 'Listen, Button,' said Shuffle. 'I've thought of a trick or two, not magic, you understand, because I wouldn't know better magic than Mr Pah. But just a trick or two.'

'I'll help,' said Button eagerly.

'Well, all you've got to do is to spread the news about that the wonderful enchanter, Mr Tricky, is visiting Tiptop Village, and giving a show,' said Shuffle. 'Tuesday afternoon at half past three. Tell everyone to be there. Mr Pah will hear about it too, and he'll be along.'

'But Shuffle, what's the trick you know?' asked Button anxiously. 'You'll have to be careful. If the trick doesn't come off, you'll get into trouble!'

'Yes, I know. But I'll have to risk that,' said Shuffle. 'They're silly tricks I've thought of, really, but that's just why I think they'll take Mr Pah in. Now you go off and spread the news about Mr Tricky, Button!'

Well, everyone soon heard that the wonderful

enchanter Mr Tricky, was coming next Tuesday, and, of course, Mr Pah heard it too.

Ha! A chance to show him up! thought Mr Pah. *A chance to show how much cleverer I am than this Mr Tricky, whoever he is!*

Everyone was on the village green at half past three. Shuffle was there, too, dressed in a flowing cloak and a pointed hat. He had rubbed a whisker spell on his face, so he had a very big beard, and didn't look at all like little Shuffle!

Mr Pah came too, pahing and poohing as usual. He pushed his way to the front. 'I'm Mr Pah, the famous magician,' he said. 'I've never heard of you! There's nothing you can do that I can't. What are you going to do? What's that blackboard for?'

'I was going to teach a few spells,' said Shuffle, and he wrote down a few simple ones on the board. Mr Pah laughed till he cried.

'Sort of thing I learnt in my pram!' he said. 'You'll be teaching us that two and two make four next.'

'Well, I wasn't going to teach that, I was going to show that six and four can make eleven, not ten,' said Shuffle, his beard waving in the wind. 'Can you do that, Mr Pah?'

There was a silence, as everyone listened for Mr Pah's answer.

'Impossible, and you know it,' said Mr Pah. 'No matter how you try, six and four will only make ten, not eleven. You're a silly fellow, Mr Tricky. I'll give you a sack of gold if you can make six and four into eleven!'

'Then watch me!' cried little Shuffle, and everyone craned to see what he was putting on the blackboard.

'Now look, what's this?' asked Shuffle, and he wrote down 'VI'.

'Six!' cried everyone.

'And what's this?' asked Shuffle, and wrote down 'IV'.

'Four!' yelled everybody.

'Now watch me make six and four into eleven!'

shouted Shuffle. 'Here is my VI again – six as anyone can see – but I'm going to write my IV upside down this time, like this – ΛI – and I'll write it touching the first VI – there you are, it's now XI, and isn't that eleven?'

'Yes, it is, it is!' shouted everyone in delight. Mr Pah stared in disgust.

'A trick, that's all,' he said.

'I never said it wasn't,' said Shuffle. 'That sack of gold is mine, Mr Pah! And now another challenge, can you write a word that exactly describes you, and which reads the same upside down?'

'Impossible,' said Mr Pah grumpily. 'Never heard of one in my life!'

'Well, I learnt it at school!' said Shuffle, and on the blackboard in very large letters he wrote this word:

chump

'Chump!' gasped everyone. And they laughed and

laughed. Mr Pah turned scarlet. He glared at Shuffle, who was now solemnly turning the board the other way up. And lo and behold the word was exactly the same upside down. You try it!

Mr Pah stalked off, caught the next bus and never came back again. But he was honest enough to leave two sacks of gold pieces behind!

'You're rich, Shuffle!' said everyone. 'You're a prince! You can build a castle, and call yourself Prince Shuffle.'

'I'm sharing out the gold with everyone in the village,' said Shuffle. 'I'm no prince. I'm a village cobbler and I'm happy in my job. Come along and help me count out the money, and this time six and four will make ten, and not eleven. No tricks this time!'

So he shared out all the money, and I'm really not surprised to know that when people meet him, they call out, 'Hello, Prince Shuffle!' Are you?

The Strange Spell

The Strange Spell

ONCE UPON a time Mollie Brown had a strange adventure. She was coming home from school one autumn afternoon, her satchel in her hand, when she heard someone calling.

'Hi, little girl, hi!'

She looked all over the place, and at first she couldn't see anyone. Then, to her enormous surprise, she saw a little man waving to her from a patch of thistles nearby. He wasn't much bigger than a doll, and he was dressed in grey-green and purple, just like the thistles.

'Are you calling *me*?' asked Mollie.

'Of course I am,' said the little man. 'You go to school, don't you? They teach you to be clever there, don't they? Well, I want you to help me. If you will, I'll give you a wish that will come true.'

Mollie felt so excited that she could hardly answer. The little man beckoned her nearer, and then showed her a piece of paper.

'I've got to make this spell today,' he said, 'and I can't make it out. Please tell me if you know what all this means.'

Mollie took the paper and read it. This is what it said:

Take the stone from half a donkey's bray, and the seed from the third of a cheer. Place both together in an empty acorn cup. Fill with water, and set it out in the moonlight, when it will gradually come to the boil if the maker has done no wrong for three days. Let it cool, and stand it on your windowsill. It will bring you a year of happy days.

'How strange!' said Mollie, thinking she really must be in a dream. But she wasn't. It was all quite real.

'Take the paper home with you, and try to make out what it means,' begged the little man. 'Please!'

'All right,' said Mollie. 'But I'm not at all sure I'm clever enough to find out!'

'Come back tonight,' called the little man, and disappeared into the thistles. Mollie ran home to tea.

After tea she sat down and puzzled over the spell. *Take the stone from half a donkey's bray*. Whatever could that mean? It sounded like nonsense. *And the seed from the third of a cheer*. That didn't make any sense either. The rest seemed easy. Mollie thought and thought. Are *you* thinking too? She puzzled over the spell, and suddenly she got the first part done!

'Half a donkey's bray,' she said. 'Well, a donkey says hee-haw. Let me see – what's half of hee-haw? Either hee or haw. Haw – perhaps it's haw? Take the stone from a haw – oh, oh, that's it! The haws are ripe now, and perhaps they have stones inside like plums. I'll go and see.'

She went – and what did she find? Who knows?

Yes, each haw had a small stone in the middle. Good, that was part of the spell done. Mollie puzzled over the next bit. 'Take the seed from the third of a cheer,' she read. 'A cheer? I wonder if that means hip-hip-hurrah! That's three words. Each word is a third of the cheer – so perhaps hip is the word that is meant. Now the seed of a hip. Yes, that makes sense! The hips are ripe too, and they have hairy seeds inside them. Good! I've done it. The spell should read, "Take the stone from a haw and the seed from a hip." I'll go and find that little man!'

Off she ran. He was waiting for her in the thistles, and you should have seen his face when Mollie told him what the spell meant! He was simply delighted!

'A thousand thanks!' he said. 'Wait for the next full moon night and wish your wish. It will come true.'

So Mollie has a wish, and she is waiting and waiting for the full moon. Could *you* have helped that little man if he had called to you? I wonder!

Green-Eyes' Mistake

Green-Eyes' Mistake

GREEN-EYES was a large black cat with the biggest, greenest eyes you can imagine. He belonged to the witch Tiptap, and, like all witches' cats, he had to help her with her spells.

Green-Eyes had an easy life, for he had nothing to do except come when the witch called him, and help her to stir her magic bowl, or sit patiently inside a magic ring while she muttered spells. He had plenty of good food – fish, milk and, sometimes, cream.

He loved cream, and thought he didn't get enough of it.

'I ought to have cream each day,' he said to himself.

'I am a hard-working witch's cat, and I think my mistress should buy me at least threepenny worth of good rich cream each day. But no – she gets it once a week, and that's all. Mean creature.'

'What is the matter, Green-Eyes?' asked the witch when she saw the cat sulking in the corner.

'I think you should buy me more cream,' said the cat gloomily.

'Nonsense!' said the witch sharply. 'How dare you talk like that, Green-Eyes. You have a fine life with me – no mice to catch, nothing to do except to give me a little help sometimes. I am really ashamed of you.'

Green-Eyes twitched his fine whiskers and did not dare to say another word. But he thought a great deal. He wished and wished he could make Tiptap give him more cream, but he could not see how to do it. And then one day he had an idea.

Tiptap called him to help her with a spell. It was a strange piece of magic she was doing. She took a broken piece of china and put it into her big magic bowl. She called Green-Eyes to stir it and he did so. Then Tiptap muttered the enchanted words, and the tiny piece of china grew slowly into a beautiful little milk jug. The witch took it out of the bowl and set it on the table.

She sent Green-Eyes for a lemon from the larder. From the lemon she took a little piece of peel and one pip. These she dropped into the jug.

'Pour lemonade, little jug,' she commanded. And then, to Green-Eyes' surprise, the small jug lifted itself into the air and poured lemonade into a glass that the witch had put nearby. Green-Eyes looked into the jug in amazement. There was no lemonade there – only the pip and the bit of lemon skin hopping about. And yet the lemonade certainly came from the jug.

'This is a fine enchanted jug,' said Tiptap, pleased. 'I shall sell it to the wizard tomorrow. He is coming to call on me.'

She drank the lemonade herself, and said it was

very good. Then she took a tea leaf from her tea caddy, a grain of sugar, and a spot of milk and put them in the jug, first taking out the pip and lemon skin.

'Pour tea, little jug,' she said. And at once the jug tilted itself up and poured out a steaming hot cup of tea. There was just the right amount of milk in it, and of sugar too. Green-Eyes tasted some that Tiptap poured for him into a saucer, so he knew.

'I shall be able to sell that jug for twenty golden pounds,' said Tiptap, pleased. She set the jug on the dresser and went to wash her hands.

'I am going out to tea this afternoon, Green-Eyes,' she said. 'You must keep house for me. Sit by the fire and listen for the doorbell in case anyone comes.'

Now as soon as Tiptap had gone, Green-Eyes thought of a fine idea. If he took that jug for himself, and hid it somewhere, he could make it pour out cream for him whenever he wanted some! Oh, what a fine idea.

'But where shall I hide the jug?' wondered Green-Eyes. 'I know. I will hide it behind the bath in the bathroom upstairs. I can take my dish up there, and no one will ever know. Ho, ho. I'll have cream now whenever I want it.'

The naughty cat first of all took his dish upstairs and put it behind the bath, then he went to fetch the jug. It was difficult for him to reach, but he managed it. He pushed a chair to the dresser, jumped up on it, leapt on to the dresser and took the jug-handle in his mouth. Then, very carefully, he jumped down to the floor again and ran upstairs with the jug. The next thing to get was a drop of cream. But was there any in the larder? Green-Eyes didn't think so. Down he ran again and went to the larder.

He stood up with his front paws on the shelf and sniffed around. No, there was no cream, but wait a minute – there was a bowl of milk there, and on the top of it was a layer of cream, for the milk was very rich.

Good, thought Green-Eyes, pleased. He took a spoon and scraped off a drop of cream. Then upstairs he went once more, and emptied the spot of cream into the magic jug.

There it was, at the bottom of the jug. Green-Eyes felt excited. He spoke to the jug.

'Pour cream, little jug,' he said. At once the jug tilted itself up, and a steady stream of rich cream fell into the bowl. Green-Eyes licked it up as fast as it poured in.

And just at that very moment, the doorbell rang. 'It's only the washing come back,' said Green-Eyes to himself. 'I'll just pop downstairs and get it and then hurry back here. The bowl will be full again by then.'

So, leaving the jug still pouring cream steadily into his bowl, Green-Eyes ran down the stairs at top speed. He opened the front door, thinking to see the girl who brought back the washing – but instead he saw the wizard who often came to pay a call on Witch Tiptap.

'Is your mistress in?' asked the wizard, walking into the hall.

'No, sir, she is out to tea,' said Green-Eyes.

'Well, what a nuisance,' said the wizard. 'I want to write a letter. Where's the paper and ink?'

'In here, sir,' said Green-Eyes, running before the wizard into the little parlour. 'You will find all you want here.'

He was just running upstairs when the wizard called him. 'Ho, Green-Eyes. There is no ink in the inkstand.'

Green-Eyes did not dare to keep the wizard waiting, for he had a very hot temper. So down he ran and tore into the kitchen to get the big ink bottle. He filled the inkstand and went off again. But he was only halfway up the stairs when the wizard shouted for him again.

'What do you want to keep running off like that for? Come here. The nib in this pen is rusty.'

'Tails and whiskers, that cream will be running

over,' said Green-Eyes in a panic. 'What a mess it will make. I'll have to clear it up before Tiptap comes home.'

He ran to the kitchen drawer and got out the box of nibs that he knew was kept there. He chose one and gave it to the wizard. Then off he went again, running upstairs.

But before he could reach the bathroom the wizard called him again. 'Green-Eyes! Green-Eyes! Bless us all, why does that cat disappear like this? Doesn't he like my company? Green-Eyes, will you come here? There are no envelopes at all. How can I write a letter without an envelope to put it in?'

Poor Green-Eyes. He fled downstairs again and found the angry wizard some envelopes. He was just going to slip out of the door once more when the wizard looked at him sternly.

'Why do you keep running off like that?' he asked. 'Have you something so important to do?'

'N-n-n-n-n-no,' stammered Green-Eyes, not

knowing quite what to say.

'Then stay here,' said the wizard, beginning to write his letter. 'I'm tired of calling you whenever I want anything. Sit down in that chair where I can see you, and don't disturb me by running upstairs again.'

Green-Eyes sat meekly down in the chair. Presently the wizard became interested in his letter, and his head bent so low that his nose almost touched the paper. Green-Eyes felt quite sure he could not see him – so, very quietly, he slid out of the chair, crept out of the door on velvet paws, and shot up the stairs as if a hundred dogs were after him.

And just outside the bathroom door he saw something that made his heart sink down into his paws! Cream was leaking out under the door!

The bowl has overflowed and the cream is all over the floor! thought poor Green-Eyes. *Oh, my! What shall I do? I simply must go into the bathroom and stop that jug.*

'Green-Eyes! Green-Eyes! Bless me if that cat hasn't done his disappearing trick again!' suddenly shouted the wizard from downstairs. Green-Eyes was so startled that he fell over, rolled to the top of the stairs, lost his balance there and fell headlong down to the bottom. The wizard rushed out of the parlour when he heard the noise, and stood in amazement when he saw Green-Eyes rolling down the stairs.

'Is this a new sort of game you are playing, Green-Eyes?' asked the wizard. 'A poor sort of game, I should think! You must be covered with bruises! I want a stamp for my letter. Come and get me one, and then, stars and moon, if you move out of my sight again, I'll turn your whiskers into snakes!'

Green-Eyes shook and shivered. He got the wizard a stamp and then sat down meekly in his chair again. This time the wizard kept a sharp eye on him.

'Tell me if you feel you badly want to go and fall down the stairs again, won't you?' he said, licking the stamp. 'What an extraordinary cat you are! I wouldn't keep you for five minutes, if I were Witch Tiptap! You haven't any manners at all! Grrrrrrrr!'

He growled so much like a dog that Green-Eyes shook like a jelly, and looked round to see where the dog was. The wizard laughed.

'And now, perhaps, you will get me Tiptap's morning newspaper and let me have a look at it,' he said. 'It is raining and I shall have to wait here till it stops.'

Oh dear, oh dear, this was worse and worse! How long was the wizard going to stay? Green-Eyes felt very miserable. If only he hadn't meddled with that jug!

He fetched the newspaper, and, on his way, he glanced up the stairs. To his horror he saw that the cream was dripping from the top step to the next one! It had run out on to the landing and was now going to roll slowly down the stairs.

'Sit down again,' said the wizard. 'I am not going to have you popping in and out of the room. It is most upsetting.'

So Green-Eyes sat down. Presently a soft dripping

sound was heard. The wizard pricked up his ears. 'What's that noise?' he said.

'P-p-p-perhaps it's the k-k-k-kitchen tap dripping,' stammered Green-Eyes, not knowing what to say.

'Go and turn it off then,' said the wizard. 'A dripping noise annoys me.'

Green-Eyes shot out of the door, meaning to go upstairs and get the magic jug – but the wizard heard him going upstairs and roared at him.

'Does your kitchen tap live upstairs? Go into the kitchen and turn it off!'

So Green-Eyes went sadly to the kitchen – but, of course, the tap was not dripping. Then he went back to the parlour and once more sat down.

The dripping noise went on. The wizard heard it and looked at Green-Eyes. 'Was the kitchen tap dripping?' he asked.

'No, it wasn't,' said Green-Eyes. 'P-p-p-perhaps it's the kettle b-b-boiling over on the stove!'

'Go and see,' ordered the wizard. Green-Eyes

went, and outside the door he paused. Yes – he would tiptoe up the stairs and see if he could do it without being heard. But the wizard had ears like a hare and he shouted at once. 'Don't you know your way to the kitchen?'

And Green-Eyes sighed and went into the kitchen – but, of course, there was no kettle boiling over. He went back, looking very miserable – for he had seen that the cream had now dripped to the bottom step! The stairs were running with the rich yellow cream – what a mess!

'I can still hear that dripping noise,' said the wizard crossly. 'But I suppose it must be the rain.'

Green-Eyes said nothing – and then he saw something that made his fur stand up on end! Cream was creeping in under the door! Yes, it really was. It had spread over the hall and had made its way to the parlour. Green-Eyes looked at it and didn't know what to do. So he sat there and just said nothing at all. The wizard read his newspaper, keeping an eye on

Green-Eyes all the time. Presently the cream reached his big feet. The wizard shuffled them about and the cream swirled round. Green-Eyes began to shiver with fright.

The cream grew deeper and the wizard felt that his feet were cold. He looked down – and when he saw the cream all round him, he jumped to his feet in fright and astonishment.

'What is all this!' he roared. 'What is it? Why, it is cream! Is this a joke, you wicked cat? You have been behaving strangely all the afternoon – creeping away, falling down the stairs – and now comes this cream into the room! What have you been doing?'

'Oh, sir, forgive me!' wept the frightened cat. 'I stole a magic jug of Tiptap's just before you came in, and took it up to the bathroom to hide it. Just as I made it pour cream into my bowl, the bell rang, and you came. I haven't been able to go upstairs to get the jug and stop it from pouring out cream – and so the cream has come downstairs and spread everywhere! Oh, whatever shall I do?'

The wizard looked at the cat and then at the cream. Then he began to laugh. What a laugh! It shook all the ornaments on the mantelpiece!

'Well, it certainly has its funny side,' he said. 'First of all, go upstairs and stop the jug pouring out cream. Then come down again.'

Green-Eyes waded out of the room through the cream and up the stairs. He waded to the bathroom, and sure enough, there was the little magic jug, still pouring away for all it was worth!

Green-Eyes put out his paw and caught hold of it. He shook it twice, as he had seen the witch do, and it stopped pouring at once. Green-Eyes went downstairs again with the jug.

'Oh, so that's the jug, is it ?' said the wizard. 'I'll get Tiptap to sell it to me. Now, Green-Eyes, set to work, please. I don't like my boots all messy like this. Lick them clean. You like cream, don't you? Well, this will be a treat for you! My word, you'll have enough cream to last you a year!'

Green-Eyes licked the cream off the wizard's boots. It tasted dreadful mixed with boot polish. Then the wizard said goodbye, took his letter with him and went out of the door, still laughing.

But poor Green-Eyes was left to clear up the creamy mess before his mistress came back! How he worked, poor thing! He found a mop and a broom, and took the biggest pail. Then he began to clean up the cream – and in the middle of his work Tiptap came back!

She stood in the kitchen and looked into the hall and up the stairs. She guessed at once what had happened. But Green-Eyes confessed too, and soon Tiptap knew everything.

'You are a very naughty, silly, *foolish* cat,' she said sternly. 'I have a good mind to turn you into a mouse for a month.'

'Oh, no, mistress, not that!' cried Green-Eyes at once. 'I might be caught by a cat!'

'You probably would,' said the witch severely. 'And I'm not sure it wouldn't serve you right. But you are sometimes useful to me, so I will not do that. Collect all the cream into pails, dishes and bowls, Green-Eyes, and you shall have it every day until it is used up. Magic must not be wasted – and you seem so fond of cream that I am sure you will enjoy it!'

Poor Green-Eyes! He worked hard all the rest of the day, collecting the cream into dishes and pails. There were four pails full, and seven dishes, so you can guess what a lot there was. Green-Eyes had to wash all the floors and clean up the stair carpet too. He was very tired when he had finished. He went to the larder to get himself some milk – but Tiptap stopped him.

'No, Green-Eyes,' she said. 'Milk is not good enough for you, is it! You must have cream! You may have a dish of the cream.'

'But I don't want it. I've turned against cream, somehow,' said Green-Eyes.

'Oh, I can't have it wasted,' said Tiptap at once. 'You must have the cream, my dear cat, or nothing at all.'

So Green-Eyes lapped up a dish of the cream – but oh, how he hated it! Then he went to bed. He dreamt of cream and the dishes too, standing in a row on the kitchen floor! It made him feel ill to see them.

The cream turned sour – but still Green-Eyes had to lap it up, for Tiptap meant to teach him a lesson. He groaned and grumbled – but not until he said that never again would he take anything that wasn't his, did Tiptap forgive him.

'Well, if you really mean that, I'll forgive you,' she said. 'You need not finish up the cream. Go and empty it away, for it really smells dreadful now. Let this be a lesson to you, Green-Eyes. I will say no more about it.'

She kept her word – but, oh dear, whenever the wizard came to see Tiptap, how he teased Green-Eyes!

'What's that dripping noise?' he would say. 'Oho,

Green-Eyes, have you ever heard that dripping noise again? When are you coming to tea with me? I'll have CREAM for a treat. Would you like that? What! You don't like cream? Well, well, well, what a surprising cat you are!'

Then Green-Eyes would slip away to a corner, and remember the dreadful cream-day – and from that day to this he has been a good and honest little cat. So perhaps it wasn't a bad thing after all!

Now Then,
Make-a-Fuss!

Now Then, Make-a-Fuss!

ONE DARK windy evening the little wizard Make-a-Fuss went out to collect some night toadstools for his spells.

'You'd better not go,' said his wife, Selina. 'The wind will blow your cloak all the time, and try to pull off your tall, pointed hat – and you'll be in such a bad temper when you come home!'

But Make-a-Fuss wouldn't listen to Selina. He never did. He went off with his basket, and at once the wind pounced down on him in glee, tugging at his cloak as if it had hands!

He had to hold on tightly to his hat too, because it

was such a big, pointed one that the wind would dearly have loved to swish it away and play with it.

'Bother this wind!' said the wizard crossly. 'What with carrying my basket, holding my cloak round me, and keeping my hat on my head, I need another pair of hands. Shall I make myself a second pair? No – I can't quite remember the spell. I might make myself two or three more feet instead, and that would be a nuisance.'

He picked his night toadstools – very special ones, striped with red and spotted with blue. He found it very difficult to pick them while holding on to his cloak and hat at the same time, but somehow he managed. Soon his basket was full.

He began to struggle home, feeling crosser and crosser. 'Stop it, wind!' he yelled. 'You'll have my cloak off in a minute! Be still, can't you! I'm getting so cold with all your bluster and blow!'

'Wheeeeeeee!' shouted the wind and swooped down on him again, trying its hardest to pull off his hat. He went on his way, grumbling and fussing, but as there was no one to hear him, it didn't matter!

Just as he came near his front gate the wind came round a corner at top speed and blew off his big pointed hat. Away it went into the darkness, and Make-a-Fuss yelled in anger.

'You've got my hat! Bring it back at once! Do you hear me, wind? How dare you do such a thing?'

But the wind had gone on its way, and taken the hat high up in the air. You'll never guess where it put it! Right on the top of the wizard's chimney pot! It fitted it beautifully. The wind fussed round it, trying to blow it off again, but it couldn't. It fitted too tightly!

Make-a-Fuss went indoors and, dear me, what a fuss he made! 'The wind took my hat! It's loosened the buttons on my cloak! It's blown my beard all crooked, I'll have to comb it straight. It's – it's – it's—'

'Now don't make such a fuss, dear,' said his wife. 'We'll buy you another hat, and I can sew the buttons on your cloak, and here's your comb. Dear, dear, dear – you *are* a fusser!'

'What's the good of buying me another hat? That's a magic hat, you know it is,' said Make-a-Fuss. 'I can't do without it!'

'Now sit down and have your supper,' said Selina, and pushed the black cat out of his chair. 'Draw up to the fire, you look cold.'

'The chimney's smoking,' complained Make-a-Fuss, as a puff of smoke blew out into the fireplace. 'Pooh – this is horrid. Why don't we get the chimney swept?'

'But the sweep only came yesterday, you know he did,' said Selina. 'He swept it beautifully and you should have seen the soot he got down!'

'Well, he *didn't* sweep it properly,' said Make-a-Fuss, as another puff of smoke blew into his face. 'How can I sit here in this smokey room all night long because that sweep didn't sweep the chimney properly?'

'Now don't make a fuss,' said Selina. 'I tell you, the chimney *can't* be sooty now. I expect it's just smoking because it's a windy night.'

But it wasn't smoking because of the wind – it was smoking because the wizard's hat was sitting firmly on the chimney pot, preventing all the smoke from going up into the air! As soon as the smoke reached the hat, it was forced back down the chimney again and puffed out into the fireplace!

The wizard made a terrible fuss and coughed and spluttered till Selina couldn't take his nonsense any more.

'Oh, don't be so *silly*!' she said. 'Grumbling and groaning and saying such dreadful things about the poor sweep. Even if he were here he couldn't do anything. I tell you he took all the soot away!'

'Ha – so you think he couldn't do anything if he *were* here, do you?' said Make-a-Fuss. 'Well, we'll just see. I'll get him here and tell him what I think of him.' He picked up his long silver wand and waved it to and fro, shouting out such powerful magic words that the cat trembled and went to hide in a corner.

There was a sudden knock at the door. 'That's the sweep!' said Make-a-Fuss, pleased. 'My word – my spell got him here quickly, didn't it! COME IN!'

The door opened and in came a most surprised sweep – but without his brushes, of course, because he had been swept away so very suddenly from his house by a magic wind, which set him down firmly on the wizard's doorstep.

'Ha! There you are, you miserable sweep!' said the wizard. 'Now, look at this smoking chimney! You won't dare to tell me you swept it clean yesterday when you see how it's puffing out smoke!'

'Indeed, sir, I *did* sweep it clean,' said the sweep angrily. 'And what's more, the brush came out of the top of the chimney pot, as your wife will tell you! There's not a speck of soot in that chimney, sir. It must be something else blocking it.'

'Well, just you tell me what it is!' shouted Make-a-Fuss. 'Climb up on the roof and look down the chimney!'

The sweep went out of the house and gazed up at the roof. The chimney pot looked most peculiar. Whatever *was* that on the top of it – something long and pointed! He waited till the moon came out from behind a cloud – and then he suddenly saw what it was.

'The wizard's hat! Yes – it really is! However did it get there?' he cried, and rushed back into the house.

'Well – did you find out what's making the chimney smoke?' demanded Make-a-Fuss.

'Yes, I did,' said the sweep. 'And it's something *I* didn't put on the chimney. The thing that is blocking the chimney, sitting right on top of it, is *yours*, Mr Make-a-Fuss! Ho, ho! Yes, it belongs to *you*! And if you want me to fetch it down, you've got to pay me one whole pound in gold, for getting me here at this time of night, because of something that's your own silly fault!'

'Don't talk to me like that,' said Make-a-Fuss, 'else I'll turn you into one of your own brushes and sweep the chimney with you. What do you mean by all this rigmarole? *What's* on top of the chimney? I'll come and see!'

So out he went with the sweep, and his wife followed too. 'Oh! Make-a-Fuss, look, it's your HAT!' she cried. 'Oh my – there's a peculiar thing! The wind took your hat and set it down on your chimney pot –and so the smoke couldn't get out and puffed into the room instead! Oh, I really must go indoors and laugh and laugh and laugh! What*ever* will you do next?'

'I did *not* do it. The wind did,' said Make-a-Fuss, quite taken aback. 'Er – I'm sorry, sweep, that I said what I did. Here's a pound in gold. You know where the ladder is, don't you?'

It wasn't long before the sweep was up on the roof and took the hat off the chimney. At once the smoke belched out, and no more puffed into the room below.

The sweep put the wizard's hat in the hall and went home, delighted with his gold pound. Make-a-Fuss was very quiet indeed that evening and didn't make a single fuss about anything at all.

But next day when he put his hat on, what a to-do there was! 'Look at my hat! It's as black as soot! What's happened to it? Has it been in the coal cellar?'

'No, dear. It's been sitting on the chimney pot – have you forgotten?' said Selina. Well, the wizard hadn't anything to say to that, of course! He borrowed his wife's hatpin when he went out that morning in the wind. He wasn't going to have his hat up on the chimney again!

The Surprising Broom

The Surprising Broom

BENNY AND Anna had both been naughty. They had been rude and disobedient, and their mother was very cross with them.

'You are not at all nice children lately,' she said. 'You don't try to help me in any way. I am very angry with you. You want a good punishment!'

Now their mother hardly ever punished them, so Benny and Anna didn't feel at all upset. They didn't even say they were sorry.

'I've got to go out and do some shopping,' said Mother. 'You two can really do some hard work for me for a change. You can take the big broom and sweep out the yard. It is full of bits and pieces and I haven't time to do it.'

'Oh, Mother! We do hate sweeping,' said Benny grumpily. But Mother for once took no notice. She picked up her basket and went out to do her shopping.

The two children looked at one another sulkily. 'You have the first sweep,' said Anna.

'That's just like a girl!' said Benny. 'No – you're the bigger of us two. You begin first.'

'Benny! Don't be mean!' cried Anna, and she shoved her brother hard. Then, of course, there was a quarrel, and in the middle of it a funny old lady came by and watched from over the yard fence.

'What's the matter?' she called.

The children stopped fighting for a moment and looked at the old woman.

'Our mother says we are to sweep the yard and we don't want to,' said Benny. 'It's hard work. I think Anna ought to begin as she's the bigger one – and she says I ought to because I am a boy!'

'Dear, dear!' said the old lady. 'Is it such hard work to sweep a little yard like this? Well, well – if you like to give me some coins out of your moneybox, I will sell you a spell that will make the broom sweep the whole yard by itself.'

Well, you can guess that Benny and Anna were surprised to hear that! A spell! What fun! They ran to get their moneyboxes at once. Benny had threepence in his and Anna had sixpence in hers. Nine pennies altogether.

They gave the money to the old woman. She picked up the broom and rubbed some yellow stuff on it, muttering some strange sounding words as she did so. Then she smiled a funny smile, nodded her head, and went off down the road, her green eyes twinkling brightly.

The broom leant against the fence. It grew a little head at the top and winked at Benny.

'Look at that, Anna!' said Benny excitedly. 'Hey, broom – do your work. Sweep, sweep, sweep!'

The broom stood itself up. The little head nodded and grinned. It really was a very wicked-looking head! And then the broom began to sweep.

My word, how it swept that yard! It was marvellous! It swept it far, far better than the children would have done. Anna and Benny were delighted.

'That's right! Sweep up all the rubbish!' shouted Benny, dancing about for joy. It was such fun to see a broom sweeping all by itself with nobody holding it at all.

The broom began to whistle as it swept. The little head pursed its funny lips and a cheery, magic-sounding tune came from them in a whistle as clear as a blackbird's.

'Sweeeeeeep, sweeeeep, sweeeep!' went the broom all over the yard. Dust was swept up, paper was cleared into a heap, bits and pieces went into a neat pile. The job was soon done, I can tell you!

'Thank you so much, broom,' said Anna, pleased. 'Now you can have a rest. You've done well.'

The broom looked at Anna and then at Benny, and went on whistling its funny little tune. It didn't seem to want a rest. It swished itself over towards Anna's doll's pram, and swept it right over on to its side. The dolls fell out and all the blankets and rugs fell out too. The broom swept the whole lot over to the pile of dust.

Anna gave a scream. 'Oh! You wicked broom! You've knocked my pram over! Stop sweeping away my poor dolls!'

But the dolls were now on the top of the dust pile! Then the broom scurried over to where Benny had put his toy fort and soldiers. Crash! Over went the fort and down went all the soldiers – and off they were swept to the dust heap.

It was Benny's turn to be angry then – but the broom didn't seem to care at all. It just went on whistling and sweeping, its little head nodding and smiling all the time.

It went to the dustbin. It swept hard against it and

over it went. The lid went rolling across the yard with a clatter. Everything fell out of the dustbin at once!

Then the broom had a wonderful time! It swept everything up – ashes, tin, broken bottles, bits of cabbage, old tea leaves – and what a fine pile it made! Then it swept up the dustbin too, rushed across to the lid and swept that up as well.

After that the broom went quite mad. It hopped to the kitchen door and swept up the mat there. It went inside the kitchen and swept all the saucepans and kettles off the stove. They made a tremendous clatter as they rolled across the yard to the dust heap, with the broom sweeping madly behind them, whistling its silly little song all the time!

Then it swept the chairs out of the kitchen too, and the cat's basket as well – with the cat inside! Puss was so terrified that she didn't jump out until the basket was falling down the step. The broom tried its best to sweep her up, but the cat fled away over the fence.

'Oh, stop, stop, you wicked broom!' yelled Benny. But it was no good – the broom didn't stop. It just went on and on sweeping things out of the kitchen. When it tried to sweep all the things off the dresser, Anna was frightened. Whatever would Mother say if she came home to find half her cups and saucer and plates broken?

'Benny! You must stop the broom!' cried the little girl in dismay.

Benny rushed over to the broom. Anna followed. Benny tried to catch hold of the handle, but the broom dodged cleverly. Benny tried again. The broom swung itself round and rapped Benny hard on the knuckles.

'Oooh!' yelled Benny. 'You horrid thing! Wait until I catch you!'

But that's just what Benny couldn't do! The broom wasn't going to be caught just as it was having such a marvellous time. No, no! It was too much to ask.

So it dodged and twisted and got in some more little raps on Benny's hands and legs. Benny was so angry that he rushed round and round and round after the broom and got so giddy that he couldn't see where he was going.

He bumped right into Anna and they both fell over, bump! The broom gave them each a good whack – and then, my goodness me, it began to sweep them up!

Over and over went the two children, rolling towards the dust heap. The broom was so strong that they couldn't even get up! They yelled and howled but the broom took no notice. It wanted to sweep, and sweep it did!

Just as Benny and Anna rolled to the dust heap their mother came in at the gate. At once the broom became still and quiet, and leant itself against the fence. Its funny little head disappeared. It was a broom as good as gold.

'Benny! Anna! What in the world do you think you are doing?' cried their mother. 'Get up at once. And goodness me – why have you taken all the mats and chairs and saucepans out here? Did you mean to throw them away? You bad, naughty children, what a mess the yard is in!'

Benny and Anna picked themselves up, dusty and dirty, their faces tear-stained and their hair untidy. They were both crying.

'Mother! It wasn't our fault. It was that horrid broom!' wept Anna. 'It's grown a little head – and it began to sweep everything up, even us! We couldn't stop it.'

Mother looked round at the broom. It had no head now. It was a good, quiet, well-behaved broom, leaning against the fence. Mother was very angry.

'I don't know how you expect me to believe fairy tales about my broom growing a head and sweeping things out of my kitchen! It's never behaved like that with *me!* You are disgraceful children. Go straight indoors and up to bed!'

Mother went indoors with her shopping bag. The children followed her, crying. Just as they were going into the kitchen, a voice called them. They turned and saw the old woman who had rubbed the spell on the broom.

'That broom will always be ready to sweep you up if you don't behave yourselves!' she called. 'Just you be careful now!'

So they are being very careful – and all I hope is that I'm there if they begin to be bad again, because I *would* love to see that broom going mad and sweeping up Anna and Benny, wouldn't you?

The Untidy Pixie

The Untidy Pixie

THE PIXIE Twinks was always in trouble. She was so dreadfully untidy! She had buttons off her shoes, hooks off her dresses and holes in her stockings and her gloves. She had an untidy mind too – she was always leaving her things about, dropping her handkerchiefs and losing her purse.

Now one fine morning, as she was going along the road, she met Dame Hurry-By. She was in a great hurry and she called to Twinks.

'Twinks! I want to catch the bus and I haven't time to go home and put this spell in my cupboard first. Will you take it for me?'

'Yes,' said Twinks, and she held out her hand for the tiny spell, which was like a little blue pill.

'Thank you!' said Dame Hurry-By. 'Put it on the third shelf of the cupboard, Twinks. I'll find it there when I come back!'

Twinks went on to the village to do her shopping. She had her basket with her, for she had a lot of things to buy. She had actually made out a list of things she wanted, so she felt rather pleased with herself.

She came to the shops. Now, what was on her list? She looked in the basket for it – it wasn't there. It wasn't in her hand or in her pockets either. Bother! She must have left it at home! Twinks was cross with herself.

She did her shopping as best she could, trying to remember everything she wanted. Then she went home – and, of course, she quite forgot all about the spell that Dame Hurry-By had asked her to leave on the third shelf of her cupboard!

Well, when Dame Hurry-By got back that

afternoon she went straight to the shelf in the kitchen cupboard and looked for her spell – and it wasn't there! So she ran to Twinks's house at speed. 'Twinks! Twinks!' she cried. 'Where's that spell you said you would leave at my house for me?'

'Oh, my goodness!' said Twinks in dismay. 'I forgot all about it, Dame Hurry-By!'

'Well, please give it to me,' said Dame Hurry-By. 'I want it.'

Twinks stared at Dame Hurry-By and went red.

'Let me see now,' she said, 'wherever did I put it when you gave it to me?'

'In your basket, I should think,' said Dame Hurry-By. They went to look – but it wasn't there. There was a hole in the basket, and Dame Hurry-By pointed to it.

'It might have fallen out there,' she said. 'Good gracious me, Twinks, why don't you mend the basket? You'll have that hole getting bigger and then half your shopping will fall out!'

'I may have slipped the spell into one of my gloves,' said Twinks. 'I had them on this morning.'

She went to fetch her gloves. Dame Hurry-By took each one and shook it – but the spell wasn't there.

'Each of your gloves has two holes in,' she said severely. 'You should be ashamed of yourself, Twinks! The spell would certainly have fallen out of either of these. Do you think you put the spell into any of your pockets?'

'Feel,' said Twinks, so Dame Hurry-By felt – and, will you believe it, there was a hole in each of Twinks's pockets! Wasn't it dreadful! Dame Hurry-By looked sterner than ever.

'Well, if you put my spell into any of these pockets it would certainly have been lost,' she said. 'You are the most untidy, careless pixie I have ever met, Twinks!'

Twinks began to cry, but Dame Hurry-By didn't look any less cross.

'It's no use crying,' she said. 'I feel cross because

that was a very important spell. Now think hard – is there anywhere else where you might have put that spell of mine?'

'Well, I do sometimes put my handkerchief into my stocking to keep it safe when my pockets have holes in,' said Twinks. 'Maybe I put your spell into one.'

So she took off her stockings and Dame Hurry-By looked through each one – and her frown got even bigger.

'A ladder all down the back of this stocking – and, dear me, three holes in the toe of this one,' she said. 'Do you *ever* do any mending, Twinks?'

'Not often,' said Twinks. 'Oh dear, I'm so sorry about the lost spell. Do forgive me.'

'No – I shan't forgive you,' said Dame Hurry-By. 'It cost a lot of money. You must pay me for it, Twinks.'

'But I haven't any money,' sobbed Twinks. 'I've spent it all on my shopping this morning. I've only got three pennies left in my moneybox.'

'Well, what are you going to do?' asked Dame

Hurry-By sternly. 'You've got to pay me for that lost spell somehow!'

'Perhaps I'd better come and do a little work for you,' said Twinks. 'I could come every day till you think I've paid for the spell.'

'Very well. Come tomorrow,' said Dame Hurry-By. 'And don't let me see you coming with any buttons off or holes in your stockings, Twinks. I won't have people looking like that in *my* house!'

So Twinks spent the rest of the day mending her clothes, and then the next morning she set off to Dame Hurry-By's house with a big apron rolled up under her arm. Dame Hurry-By set her to work. She had to wash up the breakfast things and then do the day's washing.

Dame Hurry-By did have sharp eyes! 'Look at this cup!' she said to Twinks. 'It's so badly washed that there is still some sugar left in it! And look at that plate – you haven't even washed the mustard away!'

Twinks had to do a lot of work again – and Dame

Hurry-By was even more particular over the washing! She made Twinks wash some curtains three times before she said they were really clean! And when Twinks tore one she had to mend it as soon as it was ironed. My goodness – things were done at once in Dame Hurry-By's house, I can tell you!

Twinks grew very neat and clean herself. She was afraid of Dame Hurry-By's sharp eye and sharper tongue, and she looked anxiously each morning before she went to Dame Hurry-By's to see if all her buttons were on, and her dress neat and her stockings without holes. Soon she grew quite proud of her smart look, for she was a pretty little pixie who had really spoilt herself by being so untidy.

'Do you think I've paid for that lost spell yet?' she asked Dame Hurry-By one morning.

'Yes,' said Dame Hurry-By. 'And I'm going to give you a silver shilling for yourself, because you have got so much better lately. Here it is – put it into your purse and DON'T lose it, Twinks!'

Twinks got out her little purse and opened it – and whatever do you suppose she saw inside? Guess!

Yes – the lost spell! The little pixie had put it there to be safe, when Dame Hurry-By had given it to her a week or two back. It was the only place she hadn't thought of looking in! Silly Twinks!

'Oh, look, Dame Hurry-By!' said Twinks. 'Here's the spell after all! I had it all the time, quite safely! Oh, how foolish I am!'

'Well, you may still be foolish but you are no longer careless and untidy!' said Dame Hurry-By, with a laugh. 'Here is your silver shilling. Run off home now, and don't forget all the things you've learnt from me!'

Twinks hasn't forgotten them yet – you should see her mending her stockings each week, and sewing on buttons! It was a good thing she thought she had lost that spell, wasn't it!

Acknowledgements

All efforts have been made to seek necessary permissions.

The stories in this publication first appeared in the following publications:

'The Enchanted Bellows' first appeared in *Sunny Stories for Little Folks*, No. 97, 1930.

'Mr Tweeky's Magic Pockets' first appeared in *Sunny Stories for Little Folks*, No. 91, 1930.

'Lambs' Tails' first appeared as 'Lambs-Tails' in *The Teachers World*, No. 1600, 1934.

'The Little Bear's Adventure' first appeared as 'The Golliwog and the Duck' in *Sunny Stories for Little Folks*, No. 159, 1933.

'The Dumpy-Witch's Garden' first appeared in *Sunny Stories for Little Folks*, No. 176, 1933.

'You'd Better Be Careful, Stamp-About!' first appeared in *Enid Blyton's Magazine*, No. 25, Vol. 5, 1957.

'The Spell That Went Wrong' first appeared in *The Enid Blyton Nature Readers*, No. 12, published by Macmillan in 1945.

'The Goat, the Duck, the Goose and the Rooster' first appeared as 'The Goat, the Duck, the Goose and the Cock' in *Sunny Stories for Little Folks*, No. 113, 1931.

'The Goblin Looking Glass' first appeared as 'The Goblin Looking-Glass' in *Sunny Stories for Little Folks*, No. 176, 1933.

'The Singing Saucepan' first appeared in *Sunny Stories for Little Folks*, No. 129, 1931.

'Dame Crabby's Surprise Packet' first appeared in *Sunny Stories for Little Folks*, No. 168, 1933.

'The Very Beautiful Button' first appeared in *Sunny Stories for Little Folks*, No. 120, 1931.

'The Escape Spell' first appeared as 'The Strange Spell' in *The Teachers World*, No. 1776, 1937.

'Too-Tiny, the Gnome' first appeared as 'Too-Tiny, the Dwarf' in *Sunny Stories for Little Folks*, No. 115, 1931.

'The Magic Sweetshop' first appeared as 'The Magic Sweet Shop' in *Sunny Stories for Little Folks*, No. 194, 1934.

'The Tale of Higgle and Hum' first appeared in *Sunny Stories for Little Folks*, No. 125, 1931.

'Slip-Around's Wishing Wand' first appeared as 'Slip-Around's Wishing-Wand' in *Enid Blyton's Sunny Stories*, No. 108, 1939.

'Mr Pink-Whistle's Cat is Busy' first appeared in *Enid Blyton's Magazine*, No. 1, Vol. 3, 1955.

'The Goblin's Toyshop' first appeared in *Enid Blyton's Sunny Stories*, No. 482, 1950.

'Hooray for Shuffle the Shoemaker!' first appeared as 'Hurrah for Little Rubbalong!' in *The Evening Standard*, No. 38, 1949.

'The Strange Spell' first appeared in *The Teachers World*, No. 1581, 1933.

'Green-Eyes' Mistake' first appeared in *Sunny Stories for Little Folks*, No. 247, 1936.

'Now Then, Make-a-Fuss!' first appeared in *Enid Blyton's Magazine*, No. 10, Vol. 5, 1957.

'The Surprising Broom' first appeared in *Enid Blyton's Sunny Stories*, No. 250, 1941.

'The Untidy Pixie' first appeared in *Enid Blyton's Sunny Stories*, No. 67, 1938.

Also available:

Enid Blyton

STORIES OF
MAGIC
AND
MISCHIEF

30
stories

A spellbinding selection of magical and
mischievous tales by the world's
best-loved storyteller!

Enid Blyton

STORIES OF

ROTTEN RASCALS

30 stories

Meet some hair-raisingly horrid children in these classic stories from the world's best-loved storyteller!

ENIDBLYTON.CO.UK
IS FOR PARENTS, CHILDREN AND TEACHERS!

Sign up to the newsletter on the homepage for a monthly round-up of news from the world of

Enid Blyton

is one of the most popular children's authors of all time.
Her books have sold over 500 million copies and have
been translated into other languages more often than
any other children's author.

Enid Blyton adored writing for children. She wrote over
700 books and about 2,000 short stories. *The Famous Five*
books, now 75 years old, are her most popular. She is also
the author of other favourites including *The Secret Seven*,
The Magic Faraway Tree, *Malory Towers* and *Noddy*.

Born in London in 1897, Enid lived much of her life
in Buckinghamshire and loved dogs, gardening and the
countryside. She was very knowledgeable about trees,
flowers, birds and animals.

Dorset – where some
of the Famous Five's
adventures are set –
was a favourite place
of hers too.

Enid Blyton's
stories are read
and loved by
millions of children
(and grown-ups)
all over the world.
Visit enidblyton.co.uk
to discover more.

Illustration by
Laura Ellen Anderson.